PIPPA PARK
CRUSH AT FIRST SIGHT

PIPPA PARK
CRUSH AT FIRST SIGHT

Erin Yun

Fabled Films Press
New York

Published by Fabled Films LLC, New York

ISBN: 978-1-944020-80-4
Library of Congress Control Number: 2021953309

First Edition: September 2022

1 3 5 7 9 10 8 6 4 2

Cover Designed by Jaime Mendola-Hobbie
Jacket Art by Bev Johnson
Interior Book Design by Notion Studio
Text set in Zilla Slab
Printed by Everbest in China

FABLED FILMS PRESS
NEW YORK CITY

fabledfilms.com

For information on bulk purchases for promotional use, please contact the Fabled Films Press Sales department at info@fabledfilms.com

To those who opened this book:
I am happy you returned.

1

THE BEST TIME OF
THE YEAR

25 Days Until Christmas

I didn't know what Omma was telling my older sister, Mina, over the phone, but from Mina's expression, it couldn't be good.

As I shoveled off-brand cornflakes into my mouth, Mina glanced at me from across the kitchen table. There was a disgruntled frown on her face, but since this was more or less her usual appearance, I didn't know how concerned I should be. *Mina could make sunshine seem tragic,* I reminded myself.

She caught me staring at her, and her frown deepened. She pointed at the clock on the wall. *Oops.* The school bus would be here in fifteen minutes, and I was still in my pajamas. I spooned up the last of my cereal and carried the bowl over to the sink, where Mina's husband, Jung-Hwa, was

1

setting some soup on to simmer for the evening.

"What do you think Omma is telling Mina?" I whispered. "I hope she's not asking for gift ideas for me." Mina's idea of a good Christmas gift was a six-pack of socks and flannel underwear. I, on the other hand, was hoping my mom would bring me a particular Mixxmix dress I'd been strategically bringing up in conversations.

"Oh, they're probably just comparing prices for flights," Jung-Hwa said.

My mom lives in South Korea. I was born in America, but when I was little, Omma's work visa expired and she had to go back. She decided I would have better opportunities in the U.S., so I stayed here with Mina and Jung-Hwa, and they basically raised me. I still missed Omma, though. A lot. She always comes to spend a month with us at Christmas, and I couldn't wait to see her.

"Pippa!" Mina raised her voice. "Get dressed now!"

"I'm going," I grumbled and hurried back to my room to change.

I pulled on my khaki skirt, white blouse, and Lakeview blazer in less than a minute. The good thing about wearing a school uniform is that it never takes too long to get ready. I did have to hunt down a fresh pair of knee-highs, but by the time Mina yelled my name again, I looked every bit the part of a Lakeview student.

I had been going to Lakeview, a private school, for

nearly three months now, and I still felt an electric thrill just thinking about it. Don't get me wrong—Victoria Middle School wasn't bad, but after I got a basketball scholarship to Lakeview, my life completely changed. I was on track to becoming the best basketball player in the world (and the humblest one, too), and I was also hanging around with the popular kids.

Okay, there had been some rocky patches during the last three months. It turned out, telling lies about yourself to seem rich and cool could backfire in a big way. But after coming clean about the real me and helping my team secure a major win in our first basketball game, I was finally settling in. It probably didn't hurt that I'd scored major points in our next two games either. So far we were 3–0. Now I just had to make sure I was careful and didn't wreck things.

As I checked my hair one last time in the mirror, my phone vibrated in my pocket. It was a text from my friend Buddy. Buddy went to my old school, and if there was one downside to going to Lakeview, it was not seeing him every day.

Meet you at the Lucky Laundromat party tonight, he had written. **Does Mina want me to bring anything? We have those rainbow goldfish you like.**

Mina owned the Lucky Laundromat, and tonight was its annual Christmas party.

I was about to reply when Mina called my name again,

louder this time. I grabbed my backpack from the floor and was heading for the front door when she stopped me.

"Omma wants to talk to you," she said.

"But I'm late for school," I reminded her.

"It will only be a minute. Don't worry."

Mina telling me not to worry about being late? Major red flag. I swallowed, and the cornflakes in my stomach sloshed around uneasily.

Even though Omma was 6,935 miles away, she still had an uncanny amount of control over my life. Whenever a teacher so much as shot me a dirty look, somehow Omma knew about it. So as I took the phone, I couldn't help but wonder, What had I done now?

"Omma?" I said. When she didn't immediately answer, I knew that she wasn't calling to berate me.

"Omma, are you okay?" I asked.

"Gwenchana," Omma's voice crackled from the other side of the world.

She claimed she was fine, but I knew something was up. I saw my mom so rarely that I had gotten good at deciphering the little changes in her voice.

"What's wrong?" I asked.

The silence on the other end made my heart beat faster.

"Omma?" I pressed, struggling to keep my voice even.

It had been only a short while since my mom was in a near-fatal car accident. Mina had flown to Korea to take care of her, and the laundromat had shut down for several weeks. We lost a lot of customers. But Omma had made it through all right. Or at least, I had thought so. Now my hands went slick with sweat. Was she getting worse instead of better?

"Omma, are you okay?" I asked again.

"I won't be coming for Christmas," she finally said. My grip on the phone loosened, and my fear slowly turned to indignation.

"You're not coming? But, Omma, you're always here for Christmas. It's the only time I see you. You have to come."

My mom started talking about the cost of traveling and the fact that she was still in a hip-high cast from the accident, but I could barely pretend to listen. She started to apologize, but I didn't want to hear her say sorry. I just wanted her here.

Mina plucked her phone from my hands. "You'll miss the bus," she said. "We'll talk about this later."

I opened my mouth, but before I could get out a word, she held up a hand and said, "Later." Her voice was so steely; I knew it was no use protesting. As I stomped out of the apartment, I wondered why people always said, "We'll talk about this later" when they knew those conversations would never happen.

I reached the curb just in time to see the bus on the corner rumble away. *Perfect.* As if my morning wasn't already off to a horrible start.

I headed to the bike rack at the side of our building, dug out my key, and unlocked my ride. It was technically still fall, but it was freezing in Massachusetts. As I cycled down my street, the wind slapped hard at my face, numbed my fingers, and turned my earlobes cherry red. I hissed in a breath, clenched my hands harder around my bike's handlebars, and thought some more about Omma.

This is no big deal, I tried to convince myself. *Honestly, the holidays are overrated anyway. And Omma will come later.*

But she wouldn't be here to make *hotteok* with Jung-Hwa on Christmas day or to take Buddy and me ice-skating or even to go through my drawers and shake her head at how messy they were.

I pedaled harder, trying to escape my miserable thoughts, and turned the corner, crossing into the downtown area. Here, everything was fully decked out for Christmas. Vast swaths of artificially green garlands connected the old-fashioned lampposts, while fresh holly wreaths on every door filled the air with a sharp, wintry scent. Not to mention, there were so many lights strung up; I was surprised they hadn't short-circuited the town's electric grid. It was all so pretty, so cheerful . . . and so totally unbearable right now.

I sighed. Christmas wouldn't be Christmas without Omma.

. . .

"Push it, girls, push it!" Coach Ahmad hollered. "Give it a hundred and ten percent! And remember, you're not just running—you're in a race against yesterday's time!"

Gasping for breath, I tucked my elbows in tighter to my body and summoned up the last dregs of energy from my spent muscles. Sweat coursed down my temples and trickled into my open mouth, but I didn't let myself slow. *Give it a hundred and ten percent,* I echoed Coach's words in my mind. *Until you can't give anything else.*

Coach Ahmad blew her whistle just as I finished another lap around the gym. I skidded to a stop and immediately put my hands behind my head so that I could get as much oxygen into my lungs as possible. Somehow, it still wasn't enough.

Next to me, my friend Helen clutched her stomach and moaned. "I think I'm going to hurl."

"Just make sure to face the other way," I panted.

Coach Ahmad scanned the room. Her commanding brown eyes took in our drenched uniforms and trembling legs. I guess she decided we'd had enough torture, because she finally released us. We all staggered to the locker room, breathing hard. There were twelve of us on the team, but Helen, Starsie, Win, Bianca, and Caroline were my friends off the court, too. They were known as the Royals—the most popular group at Lakeview. I wasn't one of them—not quite. Not yet.

I tugged off my sweaty clothes and pulled on my school uniform, then slumped down onto the bench closest to my locker. Helen plopped down next to me and towel-dried her smooth brown skin. Then she handed me a water bottle. I took a grateful swig.

"Sometimes, when it gets too hard out there, I just imagine Coach Ahmad running, and all of us blowing whistles at her, and it's a lot easier," she said.

"I don't know why she's working us so hard," Win joined in. She finished adjusting the knot on her tie and tugged the golden scrunchie from her hair. All the Royals wore a golden scrunchie, either in their hair or around their wrists. It was like their logo. I know it sounds ridiculous, but I dreamed about that scrunchie. About officially becoming a Royal and wearing one, too.

"We don't have any more games till after Christmas. Winter break is in ... what? Three more weeks?" Win slumped down on the other side of me.

"Really? It's that soon?" I gnawed on the inside of my cheek, thinking about all the exams and papers I had due before then. I would definitely have to text Eliot and ask to squeeze in at least one extra math-tutoring session. Mostly because of all the work I had to turn in . . . but also because—even though I knew it was a little pathetic—I wanted to sneak in as much Eliot time as possible before I had to go cold turkey for winter break.

At the mere thought of him, my heart thumped unevenly. I had met Eliot Haverford before I met anyone else at Lakeview. He was both my math tutor and the cutest boy in the entire universe. I'd had a huge crush on him since the first day I met him, but after he made it abundantly clear that he didn't date seventh graders, I was trying to move on. So far, I was doing an okay job . . . only, did I mention how cute he was?

"Speaking of which . . ." Caroline sauntered over to us. "It's almost time for our Christmas party!"

Caroline said "our" like we had all been planning a party for weeks now, but it was the first time I had heard any mention of it. I tried not to look too concerned, but of course Caroline noticed my expression immediately.

"Oh, right, Pippa," she said. "You wouldn't know. I keep forgetting about you."

True story, I thought.

"Last year we hosted a party on Christmas Eve," Helen explained.

"*The afternoon* of Christmas Eve," Caroline corrected her. "Our parents always insist that Christmas Eve has to be

9

reserved for family." Caroline rolled her eyes.

"Right," Helen said. "Christmas Eve afternoon. We had a holiday lunch with music and cool games and other stuff. Anyway, we went all out—decorations, fancy outfits, the whole shebang. It was so much fun we decided to make it a tradition. Last year's party was at Bianca's house, but we sent out invites from the Royals."

"For the select few lucky enough to snag an invite," Caroline said.

I tried not to look too eager, but a tiny glow warmed me from the inside out. Even though I ate lunch with the Royals every day, I still felt like I was hanging on to the edges. Especially considering how rocky things had been between me and Bianca when her guard dog, Caroline, found out Bianca and I were both into Eliot. Helping my team win the game against my old school had calmed Bianca down a little. And now the Royals were including me in the Christmas party. That had to be a good sign, right? I was inching closer to the inner circle.

"Anyway, it's now the most anticipated party of the year," Helen was saying. "And this year, it's Starsie's turn to host."

"About that." Starsie shut her locker. She tugged on a strand of her freshly dyed pink hair, avoiding eye contact with any of us. "Don't hate me, but I have to bail. My parents are forcing me to go on this ski trip with them. We leave for

St. Moritz the day after school gets out. I know I should have told you guys earlier, but trust me, I'm already getting my punishment. I mean, I am so bored of Switzerland." She finally glanced up and shrugged.

I started to laugh, until I realized Starsie was being serious. Before she could notice my mistake, I quickly disguised the chuckle as a cough. Still, Win caught my glance and rolled her eyes. Both of us were on scholarships, and holiday trips to Europe weren't an option for our families. I smiled at her, glad to have someone who understood. I mean, Starsie was fun and all, but how was it even possible to get bored with an entire country?

"Anyway," Starsie swept on, "Bianca can just host the party this year, and I'll take the next two. Right, B?"

Starsie shut her locker and swung an arm over Bianca's shoulders. Bianca stiffened and her lips pressed into a tight line. Considering how sweaty Starsie's arm probably was, I couldn't blame her.

"I just wish I could be there," Starsie continued, oblivious to Bianca's pained look. "Your parties are always legendary."

"Like the gingerbread house competition last year," Helen added.

"Yeah." Starsie giggled. "There was frosting on the ceiling for a week!"

All the Royals dissolved into laughter, including

Bianca, and I didn't know whether it would be worse to stay the silent odd one out or to laugh at something when I clearly had no clue what they were talking about. I chose option C—pretending I forgot something in my locker. I didn't turn back around until I heard my name.

"Huh?" I turned to Caroline.

"I said, I can lend you a dress for the party, Pippa." Caroline gave me a smile, but her eyes weren't very friendly. "My mom got it for me. It's cute but I've never worn it, because it's like three sizes too big. Should be perfect for you."

The hairs on the back of my neck prickled with embarrassment, and for a moment, I had the urge to run over and scrutinize my hips in the big full-length mirror in the corner of the locker room. I had been eating a fair number of Choco Pies and drinking *a lot* of hot chocolate in the last week. . . . Was that why Caroline was calling me fat?

I took a deep breath and told myself to snap out of it. I wasn't fat. I was two inches taller than Caroline—of course I wore a bigger size. Besides, I had watched Mina torture herself about her weight over the years; I knew that stressing over the number on a scale wasn't worth it.

Regaining my calm, I shut my locker without even slamming it.

"Thanks so much," I said politely. "But I actually went

shopping last week. I saw an outfit I had to have, and now I have the perfect occasion!"

It was a lie that I was sure would come back to bite me at some point, but it was worth it to see the way Caroline's nostrils flared. She had been hoping for a more heated reaction from me. I honestly had no idea why. Caroline and Bianca had been slow to accept me, but ever since the game against my old school, Bianca had backed down from actively hating me. In fact, she now seemed to regard me almost with neutrality. So why couldn't Caroline leave me alone?

Starsie and Bianca finished packing up their things, and we headed out of the locker room. As Caroline and Bianca talked dresses, and Win and Starsie argued about some television show I had never seen, Helen linked arms with me.

"I need someone to hold on to," she told me. "At least until I can feel my legs again."

"I think I actually prefer not feeling them."

Helen laughed. "Wanna come over? My mom is making coconut cake for dessert."

"That sounds amazing, but my sister is throwing a holiday party. At the laundromat," I added, remembering I didn't have to hide my non-glitzy real life from the Royals anymore. "It's for the customers."

"Right," Helen said. "Buddy mentioned that."

"Oh," I said. I didn't know what else to say. It was still supremely strange to me that my best friend from my old middle school was now dating my best friend from my current middle school. But not wanting to be weird about it, I opened my mouth again, fishing for something to say.

I still hadn't come up with anything by the time we reached the parking lot.

"Anyway," Helen said, just as the silence was about to turn awkward, "tell Buddy I say hi."

"Will do."

"Oh, and make sure you say it really enthusiastically, like, 'Helen says to tell you HI!' Or . . . hmm, actually, maybe tone it down just a little." Helen tapped her chin thoughtfully. "Tell him 'hi!' with an exclamation point, but no caps. Does that make sense?"

"*Absolutely* not," Win said, looking over at us.

"What? It makes total sense to me," Starsie protested. "Clearly, it means that Helen is in l-o-v-e loooooove."

"Starsie! It's only been two dates." Helen groaned but couldn't stop smiling.

And really, I was truly happy to see my friend happy. So why was there a bizarre knot in my stomach right now? I loved Helen, and I loved Buddy, but whenever I thought about them together, it made me feel odd.

I waved goodbye to the Royals, but they were all too

preoccupied with singing, "Helen and Buddy sitting in a tree, k-i-s-s-i-n-g" to notice me.

I walked over to my bike, my thoughts returning to the Royals' Christmas party. It didn't make up for Omma not coming, but at least I had something to look forward to. And it could change my whole Lakeview life. Other kids would see me at a Royals' party, which would mean I'd have the Royals' stamp of approval.

To be honest, I'd always struggled to fit in. I definitely didn't do a great job of it in my old school, so Lakeview was my fresh start. And if the Royals liked you, everyone liked you.

And if they didn't . . . well, that was one thing I didn't think I had to worry about anymore.

2

PAST

Still 25 Days Until Christmas

I locked up my bike in front of the Lucky Laundromat as fast as anyone could with frozen fingers. I sprinted toward the entrance, already late. *Only Mina would hold a Christmas party on December 1*, I thought. Mina believed in being early—for everything. Before I could open the door, two elderly women from across the street toddled out. They each wore huge eyeglasses that took up most of their faces, but somehow they still didn't notice me.

"Not a big turnout this year," the woman on the left said.

"A shame," the one on the right agreed.

They waddled past me, and I ducked into the store.

Mina and Jung-Hwa had done a great job decorating. We couldn't afford anything high-tech, like a blow-up snowman, and we didn't have the space for something huge, like a real tree, but they had dug up all the old lights and tinsel we had, and Mina had even splurged for some fresh green holly and a shiny red "Welcome" banner. One of the guests had also brought us a new vase filled with bright winter pansies, which, while not exactly sticking to the theme, added lovely color to the room.

Money was tight, so the food budget was minimal, but there was a bowl full of shrimp crackers and another full of crispy peanut and squid balls, and Jung-Hwa had picked up a day-old pack of mince pies from the grocery store. Altogether, it was the jolliest I'd ever seen the laundromat look, despite the flickering fluorescent lighting.

Except that there were almost no guests inside. I saw Mrs. Lee, our upstairs neighbor, trying to cajole her huge Burmese cat, Boz, down from the top of a dryer, and over in another corner, the Jeongs were showing off pics of their new niece to Mrs. Wilson, but that was pretty much it.

Buddy stood with Mina and Jung-Hwa over by the snack table, hogging all the shrimp crackers, so I headed there.

"You're late, Park," Buddy said before Mina could get to it.

"I know, I know. Practice." I turned to Mina. "I thought the party was supposed to start at six."

"It did start at six," Mina said.

"Oh." Had all the customers decided to come fashionably late this year?

Feeling awkward, I swiped up a handful of shrimp

crackers before dragging Buddy away so that we could talk in private. As we headed to our usual hangout on top of the washers, I overheard Mrs. Lee asking Mrs. Wilson why her friend hadn't come to our party this year.

"It's a little sad." Mrs. Wilson sighed. "I'm sure you know that Mina was in Korea for a few weeks, helping her mother after she got into that terrible car accident."

"Horrible," Mrs. Lee agreed.

"Yes, well, the laundromat was closed so long, my friend switched to the one around the corner. She didn't think she should come to the party since she doesn't patronize this place anymore."

My stomach twisted, and I quickly hurried on, jumping up next to Buddy on top of one of the washing machines.

"So, what's new with you, Park?" he asked, stealing half the shrimp crackers from my open fist.

"Oh, nothing much." I thought about telling him that Omma wasn't coming home for Christmas, but I didn't want to talk about that right now. "The Royals are throwing a huge Christmas party, but I'm sure Helen has already told you about it."

Buddy's eyes lit up at the mere mention of Helen, and I remembered that I was supposed to pass on her message. "Oh, and, um, by the way, she says hi!" I recited obediently. "But anyways, I need to find a dress before—"

"She did?" Buddy cut me off. "Why didn't you tell

18

me sooner? How did she look when she said it?"

I rolled my eyes. "Like Helen? I don't know. She was wearing her Lakeview uniform, and she had her hair in braids."

Buddy groaned. "Come on, Park. Give me the good stuff. Did she look excited? Wistful? Like she was thinking about how awesome our last date was and was wondering when she would see me again?"

"She looked like she wanted to say hi," I said.

I wondered if Buddy was about to start chanting spontaneous haikus in Helen's honor. Luckily, at that moment Jung-Hwa rapped loudly on one of the washing machines, and the room went quiet as we turned toward him and Mina.

"Hello, everyone," Mina said, to all seven of us.

Jung-Hwa had convinced her to switch from her normal business clothes into a more festive red sweater, but she still looked like her usual no-nonsense self in black slacks and one-inch heels.

"I hope you're enjoying yourselves. I'm so happy you could make it." She smiled, but it didn't quite reach her eyes. She scanned the room, her dark glance glossing over the empty spaces. "I know times have been hard, but I couldn't ask for a better group of people to be here tonight."

She stopped speaking. The room remained silent, all of us expecting her to continue. However, in true Mina fashion, she was already done.

Jung-Hwa cleared his throat and clapped his hands

together. "Please, help yourself to as many snacks and as much soju as you want!"

As people started to chat again, Mrs. Lee came over to Mina and Jung-Hwa. They were close enough that I could hear Mrs. Lee when she said, "Personally, I can't see the appeal. Of those other laundry hacks, I mean. We all know Jiffy Laundry overcharges, and Local Laundry smells like dried-up ketchup. I'm pretty sure everyone's linens end up dirtier there. And The Laundry Shop? Please. Those hipsters are the worst of all. They make it seem like they're selling some gourmet product, when all I want is a place to wash my socks!"

Jung-Hwa laughed, and even Mina grinned a tiny bit.

"Lucky is going through hard times, but not forever," Mrs. Lee told Mina confidently. "In fact, my tarot cards confirmed it. I did a reading last night."

"Tarot cards?" Mina repeated. Although she was always polite to her elders, I could hear the skepticism in her voice.

Mrs. Lee opened her handbag and pulled out a small wooden box engraved with a full moon. Curious, I hopped off the washer and headed closer with Buddy behind me. Mrs. Lee showed us the deck, each glossy card with a different illustration painted on it, from a radiant golden sun to a bearded man holding a cup.

"I can do a personal reading for you," Mrs. Lee told Mina. "I'm still learning, so sometimes I switch a few things around, like romantic happiness with terrible tragedies. But with those things, it's often hard to tell the difference."

"That's a . . . nice offer. But we don't believe in that kind of stuff," Mina said.

She said "we," even though, personally, I didn't know enough about tarot cards to know whether I believed in them or not. I looked at Mrs. Lee.

"Those predict the future?" I asked.

"Absolutely not," Mina told me, just as Mrs. Lee said, "They certainly can."

Mrs. Lee narrowed her eyes at me and adjusted her big round glasses. "Would you and your friend like a reading?"

I hesitated. The idea sounded kind of cool, but I wasn't sure if I wanted to know my future. Of course, who knew if tarot cards actually worked?

"Sure," Buddy said, before I could decide either way. He glanced over at me with an eager grin. "Come on. It could be a laugh. Let's do it."

We both glanced up at Mina. Although she didn't seem particularly pleased, she allowed Mrs. Lee to pull us to the side. Buddy and I settled cross-legged on the floor opposite Mrs. Lee, who sat on a folding chair with another one beside her as a table.

"Who wants to go first?" Mrs. Lee peered at us. She nodded at Buddy. "I'm sure you're a brave boy."

"Sounds good to me," Buddy said. He didn't appear

nervous at all. Instead, he rubbed his hands together. "How does it work?"

"I'll be doing a three-card reading," Mrs. Lee said proudly. "Past, present, and future. Here, shuffle." She offered the deck to Buddy; he wiped shrimp cracker crumbs from his fingers before taking it. "If you have any specific questions you'd like to get answered, focus on those."

Mrs. Lee was quiet as Buddy passed the cards from hand to hand. Once he was satisfied, he handed the deck back. Mrs. Lee laid out the top three cards of the deck and flipped over the one farthest to the left.

"This represents your past," she said. We all peered down at the card. It was a foggy sky with eight stars surrounded by an equal number of circles. "The Eight of Pentacles. But it's reversed!" Mrs. Lee announced. "Usually, this card would represent confidence, but when it's flipped like this, it represents a lack of motivation." She shook her finger at Buddy. "Is this true?"

Buddy scratched the back of his neck. "I guess," he said. "I mean, I'm only in seventh grade."

Mrs. Lee turned over his next card. Two people gazed into each other's eyes, dreamy smiles on their golden faces. She didn't have to say the name of the card for me to guess the meaning.

"The Lovers," Mrs. Lee said, making Buddy's eyes widen. "Does this mean anything to you?"

He nodded so hard I thought his head would pop off. "What's the next card?" he demanded.

For someone who had agreed to do this "for a laugh," Buddy suddenly looked awfully invested.

As Mrs. Lee explained Buddy's last card, the Six of Wands, which promised success and self-confidence, I stared down at the Lovers. I knew it was silly to be jealous of someone else's tarot reading, but somehow, seeing Buddy pull the Lovers made me feel anxious. Like he had taken the card out of the deck, and now my chances of pulling it were zilch. Which was ridiculous . . . but that didn't stop Eliot's perfect smile from flashing through my mind.

"Ready, Pippa?"

I looked up. Mrs. Lee had finished with Buddy's reading, and now it was my turn. I thought about backing out—maybe the future was better left unknown—but before I could, Mrs. Lee placed the deck in my hands.

"Give that a shuffle," Mrs. Lee commanded. "And stop when it feels right."

I passed the cards back and forth between my hands. They felt heavier than they looked. To hide my nervousness, I looked over at Buddy and gave him a half smirk, like I knew this was all for play. But Buddy's face was solemn.

After a few more shuffles, I finally handed the deck back to Mrs. Lee, and she set out my three cards.

"Five of Cups," she said, flipping over the first one. She

peered over the rim of her glasses. "This could represent disappointment. Does that mean anything to you?"

I tried to keep my face neutral, but I immediately thought of Omma. How did the cards get that right?

They didn't, I told myself. People had tons of little disappointments all the time. That card was general enough to fit anyone.

But if I really believed that, how come I was so nervous about the second one?

As soon as Mrs. Lee flipped it over, I leaned my head in closer, squinting at the outline of a knight holding a star inside a circle.

"Ah, the Knight of Pentacles," Mrs. Lee said. She stared at it for so long I was sure it meant disaster. My palms started to sweat just as she opened up her purse and dug out a small white pamphlet. She quickly flipped through the pages. "Ah! Here we go. Knight of Pentacles. Sorry, there's so many cards, sometimes I just can't remember what they all mean. Let's see . . . This card represents hard work. You should be prepared to take on a lot of responsibility in your present life."

So far, two out of two. Surely, this card referred to the flood of final exams and last-minute essays just around the corner. But while I was impressed with the tarot cards, I was less concerned about my present than the next card. . . .

"What's the last card? My future card?"

That was the one that really mattered. What would I see? Riches, fame . . . true love?

With a dramatic flourish, Mrs. Lee turned over the last card. Even before I looked down at the card, I could tell it was bad: Buddy jerked back, and Mrs. Lee's mouth puckered.

"The Tower," she whispered.

I stared down at the Tower card. Jagged silver bolts of lightning struck the narrow, gray tower, and red fire shot out of the windows. But that wasn't the worst part. Unlike Buddy's dreamy lovers, the couple in this card was leaping from the top of the burning structure.

I shuddered. For a moment I felt as if I were the only one in the laundromat.

"Pippa?" Mina waved a hand in front of my face. "You squeaked. What's going on?"

Instead of answering, I motioned my chin toward the card in front of me.

"She drew the Tower for her future card." Buddy held it up for Mina to see.

"The Tower?" Mina repeated, shaking her head as she studied it.

Her gaze shifted to Mrs. Lee, who quickly shuffled the card back inside the deck.

"It's not necessarily as bad as it looks," she explained. "It *can* represent imminent destruction and catastrophe . . . but it could also simply mean change is coming her way."

Or my whole world is going to go up in flames. I stared at the card, my spine shriveling up like an old noodle left out to dry.

"I agree with Mina," I said, my voice low and unsure. I straightened my shoulders and cleared my throat. "Tarot cards are meaningless," I said, firmer this time. "They're just playing cards. A game. There's no way they can predict anything."

3

A PIPPA PARK PAGEANT

(Still) 25 Days Until Christmas

Mina, Jung-Hwa, and I were lost in our thoughts as we headed up the dingy stairs to our second-floor apartment.

I was still on edge from Mrs. Lee's tarot reading, but the scent of simmering *kkori gomtang* briefly revived me. Jung-Hwa had placed a pot of thick oxtails on the stove to simmer before he left for work that morning, and now, twelve hours later, the whole apartment smelled like pure, meaty warmth.

He washed his hands, tossed salt into the pot, and announced, "Dinner in fifteen."

I had some algebra homework, but I also knew it would be impossible for me to focus right now. Instead, I took a seat at the kitchen table next to Mina, who had begun to fill out thank-you cards for the customers who had made it to the party. Despite using the nice, thick kind of card stock, her stack was less than an inch tall.

From the stress lines on Mina's forehead, I could tell she was thinking about the laundromat's low turnout. And I knew I should have tried to comfort her, but we both had our own worries: Every time I closed my eyes, I could see the Tower card in my mind, as clearly as if Mrs. Lee were in our kitchen, turning it over in front of me. The lightning bolt. The flames. The couple leaping from the top.

I shuddered.

"Pippa . . . Pippa . . . hello?"

Mina waved a hand in front of my face.

I flinched. "Huh?"

"You haven't heard a word I said, have you?" Mina sighed, her mouth twisting in irritation. But when I didn't respond, she cocked her head. "You look pale. Are you feeling all right?"

"I'm fine."

"You're not still thinking about that ridiculous fortune, are you?"

My lack of a response answered for me. Mina rolled her eyes and set down her pen.

"Pippa, listen to me. There is only one person responsible for your future. And that's you. Besides, if you tried it again, you would pull three completely different cards."

"Potentially."

"I can't believe you're making me say this—even

if I did believe Mrs. Lee could predict the future, you heard what she said. The Tower card isn't necessarily bad. Don't overreact."

"But you have to admit, the first two cards seemed pretty accurate. Like the Five of Cups. Mrs. Lee said that represents disappointment. Isn't it a little weird that I pulled that card the same day that Omma said she couldn't make it home?"

"Just think about how many good things are happening right now," Jung-Hwa countered. He brought a large bowl of rice to the table, along with a smaller bowl of sour kimchi. "Your teachers seem very happy with your progress at school, and you said things have been going well with your new friends. Plus, I'm sure you know this, but I couldn't be prouder of my basketball star." He ran his knuckles over my head, making my hair dance with static electricity. I stuck my tongue out at him. "It's all about perspective. Come on my little *gangaji*. It's the happiest time of the year. Don't waste that."

"Maybe you're right."

I still wasn't a hundred-percent satisfied, but sitting in my warm, bright kitchen, about to consume my weight in broth, it was hard to worry.

Buzz, buzz, buzz.

I looked down at my phone as a series of quick texts came in from Helen.

Do you think I have to formally invite Buddy to our Christmas party?

Or is it more of a given?

And if I do ask him, do I do it over text?

HELP.

Do you want it to be a formal thing? I quickly texted back. *Let's talk about it at lunch tomorrow.*

Without waiting for a response, I stuck my phone back in my pocket. I felt a little bad about my answer, but I knew that the rest of the Royals would be able to help Helen with dating advice a lot more than I could. Besides, she had reminded me of something. . . .

I waited until Mina finished sealing her envelopes before clearing my throat. She glanced over at me. I tried to keep my expression completely innocent, but whatever Mina saw in my eyes made her lips purse in suspicion.

"Speaking of the happiest time of the year," I started out, trying to flood Mina's subconscious with positive images. Her lips thinned even more. I had better just get on with it. "It's been a while since we went shopping. I was thinking that maybe it'd be nice to have a new dress for the holidays." I said "holidays" instead of "Royals' party" because I figured it would sound better to Mina, but she didn't look convinced. She didn't meet my eyes as she slipped her cards into a thick black folder.

"Let's talk about this later," she said.

Great. There was that "later" thing again.

"It doesn't have to be expensive," I pressed. "Just something nice. For when special occasions pop up. You always say to dress how I want to be perceived. Besides, it could be my Christmas present."

Mina rubbed the bridge of her nose. "Please, Pippa." She sighed. "Can't you see that we're struggling right now? We can't afford presents this year, and you don't need new clothes!" Her voice started to rise.

"Well, fine. You don't need to snap." I crossed my arms.

"Come on, girls. Everyone's tired right now," Jung-Hwa soothed. He crossed over to the table and placed a steaming bowl of soup in front of each of us. I started salivating immediately—my taste buds didn't know when I was upset. "But there's nothing that kkori gomtang won't solve."

Jung-Hwa said that about a lot of foods, but in the case of oxtail soup, I thought that he might be right. It was hard to describe the taste, except that it was like the richest, beefiest thing you could imagine. The oxtail was so tender it dissolved as soon as it touched your tongue, and the saltiness of the soup was perfection combined with the spicy sourness of the kimchi and the comfort of the rice. As soon as I had my first bite, my worries melted. For a moment, it was like Mrs. Lee had never told my fortune. I had never been irritated at Mina, and the laundromat was doing great. I'd even find another way to get a new dress.

"I'm sure this oxtail wasn't cheap," Mina said. But

as soon as she tasted the soup, she, too, went silent. By the time we reached for seconds, we were both smiling.

. . .

"I might whip up some gingerbread cookies this weekend," Jung-Hwa told us after we had all eaten so much soup that our stomachs radiated heat.

"If they come out as hard and burnt as last year, we can use them to make a gingerbread house instead," I teased. Jung-Hwa was a great cook, but not a very good baker. He usually left the sweet treats up to Omma. . . .

Omma. My mood sank a little.

"Even better," he said, unphased. "We can enter it into the church's gingerbread house competition."

"Oh! That reminds me," Mina said. She turned to me, and the look in her eyes mirrored my own a few minutes ago, when I had been preparing to ask her about the dress. I put down my spoon, suspicious now, too. "Pastor Oh called— about the Christmas Pageant."

"Interesting," I said.

I looked at Mina, waiting for her to explain what this had to do with me. But she was silent. Too silent. *Oh, no.*

I shook my head. "No way."

"Come on, Pippa."

"I'm way too old to be in the pageant!"

"He's not looking for any extra sheep. The pageant has grown so large he's having trouble managing all the children on his own. He needs a couple of older kids to help out."

I shook my head in disbelief.

Pastor Oh was in charge of the Korean Baptist Church on the border between Victoria and the next town. I had attended junior youth group there a long time ago, back when Mina had forced us to go multiple times a week. But over the years, her dedication had ebbed. Nowadays, we mostly just went on special occasions, except when Omma was here. Then we went every week. It felt like forever since the last time I had participated in the pageant, but I could still remember the countless hours I had spent sweating in various animal costumes (which were washed about once every decade and smelled like it). Not an experience I cared to repeat.

"But I haven't done the pageant in years," I whined. "I don't remember any of the cues. I wouldn't be very helpful."

"Ah, the pageant. I miss those days." Jung-Hwa sighed. He dug out his phone and scrolled through photos until he brought up a slew of ancient pictures. "Look at you."

Jung-Hwa swiped though a series of photos of eight-year-old me. In some I was laughing, in some I was pouting, and in all of them I was dressed as a woolly white sheep. Well,

I was supposed to be a white sheep. In reality, the costume had taken on a dusty, dingy gray hue.

"You were so tiny back then," Mina said. Her voice softened slightly, and although most strangers wouldn't have recognized the change, it was the closest to a coo I had heard from her. "This was back before your growth spurt."

"You might not have had the lead, but you stole the show. I couldn't film anyone but you the entire time," Jung-Hwa said, proudly. "Which, incidentally, is why I wasn't allowed to volunteer to film again the next year."

I tried to maintain my resolve—NO pageant—but even I had to admit: Little me *was* pretty cute. Even if I had been going through a chunky bangs phase.

"It's for a good cause, Pippa," Mina said. I had to give her credit: She saw her opening, and she pounced. "Everyone in the community comes to the pageant. Besides"— Mina met my gaze—"Pastor Oh's influence and opinion is very valuable at the church. I ran into him at the post office the other day, and he told me that if you're willing to help him out, he'll let the Lucky Laundromat act as an official sponsor for the pageant. He'll even include a free advertisement in the program. It could help things here."

With that, I knew that Mina wasn't really *asking* me to be part of the pageant. Because if she were asking, then I would have the option to say no. But how could I when she was guilt-tripping me with the laundromat?

"Fine," I grumbled.

"Good," Mina said. It was a little short of, "Thank you, Pippa, my gorgeous, gracious, self-sacrificing little sister. What would we do without you?" but for Mina it was a lot. "The first practice is tomorrow night."

"So soon?" I groaned. "You couldn't mention that first? I'm supposed to hang out with Helen!" I hadn't spent one-on-one time with her in over a week, and now that would be even harder. Not to mention, I still had basketball practice, and it was almost the end of my first semester at Lakeview—I had to focus on my grades now more than ever. Mina should have understood that—after all, she was the one always saying it. She shouldn't force the pageant on me.

I debated refusing to go, but when I looked at Jung-Hwa, his eyes were fixed so pleadingly on me that my stomach churned. Mina and Jung-Hwa were always there for me. I had to be there for them. . . .

But that didn't mean I had to be happy about it.

"Fine," I mumbled.

I pushed away my soup bowl—even if it was more of a symbolic gesture at this point, seeing as I'd already eaten half the pot. I maintained a steady frown as I washed it, trying to look on the bright side. I didn't want to be part of this pageant, but we needed more business at the laundromat. And maybe Mina would take it easier on me now that I was doing her a massive favor. I perked up a bit. In fact, maybe she would be so appreciative she would help me out with a little something as well. Somewhere out there, my perfect dress was waiting for me. A dress that would steal hearts. A dress that would make Caroline jealous of how stunningly mature I looked. A dress that would fix everything. And it had already started working its magic—as I dreamed about how gorgeous I'd look in it, the pageant and the Tower card totally drifted from my thoughts.

4

BOYS

"Heads up, everybody." Mrs. Rogers, my algebra teacher, rapped her dry-erase marker on the whiteboard. "The last test of the semester is next Tuesday, so I suggest you pay attention."

Next Tuesday? As in exactly one week from now? "Oh, no," I groaned. I stared at the equations on the board. The numbers made about as much sense to me as Morse code.

I'm doomed, I thought. *I'll never pass this test.*

Wait. Don't panic. I took a deep breath. *I'll text Eliot and see if he's available for a couple of tutoring sessions. If he can help me, I just might do okay.*

The tension in my shoulders eased, and it also occurred to me that this test meant I'd definitely get to see Eliot at least one more time before the break.

I had to smile. On what planet would I ever think a math test was a good thing? Planet Eliot, of course.

I wondered if he would be coming to the Royals' party. Surely Bianca would invite him. Would she invite him as her date? *He doesn't date seventh graders, remember?* I reminded myself. Unless that whole seventh-grader thing had just been an excuse. . . .

Suddenly, my throat felt a little full. Did we have to bring dates to the party? Helen had already mentioned inviting Buddy. But that didn't mean he was going to be her *date* date, right? Right, I decided. She would definitely have said if it was a *date* date.

Stop worrying, I told myself. *Having a date can't be required.*

I packed up my things and headed to my locker. I quickly checked the hallway to make sure none of the teachers were around. Then I took out my phone and texted Eliot.

Unexpected test alert. Algebra exam next week. Any way we can work in another session before break?

Say yes, say yes, say yes. He had to say yes. And while we were studying, I thought, I'd do some sleuthing, and see if he was coming to the party. Date or not, he'd still see me with the Royals in my dream dress.

Before I could put my phone away, it buzzed. Eliot responded almost immediately. It made me smile to think of the two of us walking through the hallways at this very moment, both breaking Lakeview's no-texting rules.

How about Thursday afternoon? Do you mind meeting in the library?

In the library? Lakeview's library?

I didn't mind *at all* hanging out with Eliot at school. It would make me feel less like a tutoring obligation and more like a legitimate friend. And if some of the girls in my grade happened to spot us—even better! Plus, even though Eliot lived in the biggest house in town, it wasn't the best space for personal conversations. Eliot's mother had died when he was little, leaving behind a grouchy father (who also happened to be our headmaster here at Lakeview) and a beyond-creepy great-aunt who liked to snoop. Studying in the library would be much mellower.

By the time I reached my locker, Helen was already waiting for me.

"What has you all glowy?" she teased.

"Oh, nothing."

"Come on," she said.

But I didn't want to tell her that the reason I was smiling was because right now, Eliot wasn't in some other part of the school—he was here, inside my head, both of us at the Royals' Christmas party. He was wearing a tux, and I was wearing a strapless dress made entirely of diamonds . . . which, yes, were quite hard and pointy, but looked *amazing*. "I know I said I don't date seventh graders," Eliot was saying, smiling shyly.

"But I could make an exception for you." Of course, it was at that exact moment that we noticed we were standing underneath a sprig of mistletoe. . . .

"Really, it's nothing," I told Helen. "I'm just thinking that this Christmas has potential. That's all."

. . .

There was no practice today—and no school tomorrow!—on account of some training thing that all the teachers in Victoria had to attend, so during lunch Helen suggested the group head to Duo's after school to talk details about our upcoming party. Since pageant practice didn't start until six thirty, I could swing by. We decided to meet up in the parking lot after school.

During my last class, one of the girls asked a million questions about the homework, so by the time I made it to the parking lot, almost all the Royals had already piled into Starsie's car. I got there just in time to see lanky Win squeeze herself into the back of the sleek red Volvo, looking like some kind of contortionist. Only Caroline remained outside, hovering next to her mom's black Range Rover.

"See you two there!" Starsie called out from the passenger window. She waved her fingers at us as the Volvo slowly rolled away.

I looked over at Caroline, who looked over at me. Half

of me expected her to just leave me in the parking lot, but after an uncomfortable beat, she shrugged.

"I guess you're riding with me, Pippa."

I followed Caroline into the back of her mom's car, debating if it would be better to just walk to Duo's. Sure, by the time I actually got there I probably wouldn't be able to feel my fingers or toes anymore . . . but I also wouldn't have to sit in strained silence with Caroline for an entire car ride. Still, if Caroline felt uncomfortable, she didn't show it, so I guess I could deal with it, too.

"Hey, Mom," she said, tossing her backpack on the floor. "We're going to Duo's."

Caroline's voice was smooth and casually commanding, like she was speaking to a chauffeur. I couldn't imagine how Mina would react if I ordered her around in that tone, but Mrs. Bingham just flashed us a thumbs-up and continued to talk spin classes with whoever was on the other end of her Bluetooth earpiece.

I was expecting Caroline to give me the cold shoulder, but as soon as we hit the road, she started prattling on about the Christmas party. Possible guests, decorations, food. She talked so fast that even if I had had something to add to the conversation, there was no opportunity to jump in. We were halfway to Duo's before she took a breath.

"Aren't you excited, Pippa?" Caroline demanded. "You've never been to a Royals' party before. I'm sure the ones you went to at Victoria Middle were quite a bit . . . well . . . different."

In other words: bad.

Again, before I had time to respond, Caroline swept on: "Ugh. There's just so many decisions to make. Like what to wear. I bought a couple of new dresses last week, but neither of them are special enough for the party. See?"

Caroline shoved her phone in front of my face and scrolled back and forth between pictures of two different dresses. One was a rose-gold halter dress embellished around the waist with a line of smooth pearls, and the other was an off-the-shoulder, seafoam-blue dress with a dramatic slit on the left side. Both of the dresses were drop-dead gorgeous, and each looked five times as expensive as my entire wardrobe combined.

"I'll probably go shopping again tomorrow. That boutique downtown, Impressions, has some cute stuff."

Caroline continued to talk about how *hard* it was to find the perfect outfit, and how *exhausting* it was to go dress shopping all day. I "mmmed" and "oohed" absentmindedly but didn't really pay attention until Caroline said, "Have you thought about who you're going to bring?"

I stopped staring out the window.

"Excuse me?"

"As your plus-one. Duh. Every Royal gets one, and

Helen's for sure bringing Buddy." Caroline paused, like she was giving me time for that to sink in. "Not that I know what she sees in him. But whatever. Who are you going to bring?"

"Hmmmm," I said, drawing out the word to buy time. Besides Eliot and Buddy, what boys did I actually know? *None* sounded about right.

I wondered again if Bianca would ask Eliot. Even though I had told all the Royals about the "doesn't date seventh graders" thing, that didn't stop her from hanging around his locker before school, fluffing her hair, and giggling.

Caroline was still waiting for an answer, and not wanting to look like a total dork, I shrugged. "I'm still deciding. But I'm not worried."

"Bold," Caroline said. She ran a hand through her long, glossy red hair and sighed. "But relatable. I don't know who I'm going to bring, either." She paused. "Mark and Ryan are both on the boys' basketball team, but they're just seventh graders. Oliver is in eighth grade, so he might be okay. Plus, earlier today, Starsie said Josiah had a question for me, and I'm pretty sure I know what he's going to ask."

"Maybe you should just do it *Bachelorette* style and have them compete for you."

I was being sarcastic, but Caroline didn't seem to notice. "Hmm. That's actually not a terrible idea, Pippa. Wow."

Caroline listed out pros and cons for each of her suit-

43

ors, and as she did, I couldn't help but slip into a small fantasy.

I was at a ritzy department store with dressing rooms bigger than my bedroom, trying on a dozen glamorous outfits, each with silky fabric that melted through my fingers. Outside, Eliot waited, ready to help his *date* choose between dresses. Each time I emerged in a new one, he would leap out of his chair, stunned at how beautiful I looked. And he wouldn't be shy about telling me either.

I sighed a little and pushed away the fantasy. It would only make reality more disappointing, if that was even possible.

When we reached Duo's, Caroline was still bragging about her horde of devoted admirers. Although the ride couldn't have been more than ten minutes, I had never been so happy to exit a vehicle in my life.

I hadn't been to Duo's in a week or so, and Mrs. Jecknell, the co-owner, had done a nice job cozying up the place—probably against Mr. Hine's wishes. Red and green tinsel glittered from wall to wall, and the old-fashioned jukebox blasted Chuck Berry's "Run Rudolph Run." A sign above the cash register even advertised two new winter-themed treats: the "All I Want for Christmas Is a Peanut Butter Fudge Sundae" and the "Chestnuts Roasting on a Vanilla Sundae." If I had come here with Buddy, we would have ordered both and split them, but I had a feeling if I got one with the Royals, Caroline would give me that sickly sweet smile of hers and then purse her lips, like she was confirming that I would never be able to fit into her hand-me-downs.

Ugh.

The rest of the Royals had already claimed a table, so I quickly took a seat next to Helen.

"Starsie, are you okay with taking the lead on invites?" Helen was asking. She flashed me a quick smile when I sat and then continued on, "You're so great at designing them."

The rest of the girls nodded, except for Bianca, who was staring at something on her phone.

"Does that sound good, B?" Helen asked.

"Hmm?" Bianca put her phone facedown on the table, and shook her head, like she was trying to refocus. "Oh, yeah. Fine with me."

Inadvertently, my eyebrows inched up my forehead. I had assumed Bianca would be the most invested in the party planning process, but she barely seemed to be in the same room with us. Still, if anyone else noticed that Bianca was acting weird, they didn't show it.

"Come on, these are just small details," Starsie said. "Let's talk about the good stuff. Like where you're going to get your nails and your hair done. Humph. I had the perfect dress picked out. I still can't believe my parents are making me miss this!"

"We'll all be mourning for you while you master the slopes, Stars," Win said.

"Yeah, well, maybe there'll be some cuties in my ski group." Starsie perked up. "That would make things a little more interesting."

Helen and I laughed, but Caroline was all business.

"Starsie's right," she said. "We should coordinate when we're getting our nails done. Maybe the day before?"

"No can do." Win shook her head. "That's Dessert Day."

Everyone but me seemed to understand immediately. "Dessert Day?"

"It's something my family does each year," Win explained. "We wake up at like, five in the morning and spend the whole day cooking. Everyone gets one dessert choice. Then we make them all and we share. My brothers always choose something with chocolate and frosting, and my dad always wants to make *meghli*, which is a kind of Lebanese rice pudding. Anyway, it takes forever, but by the end, our whole house smells delicious."

"Well, what about that night?" Caroline pressed.

This time, Helen shook her head. "I'm driving into Boston with my parents, remember? Every December, we go see *The Nutcracker*. It's a little boring, but my mom goes nuts—no pun intended—over all the costumes."

As I listened to the Royals share all the fun things

they did each Christmas, I couldn't help but feel a little jealous. My family had its own traditions, too. Usually, they included going to church with Omma, then playing Yunnori at home. Omma would make hotteok, and sometimes Jung-Hwa and I made star-shaped *dalgona*, heating white sugar in a ladle over the stovetop, and stirring in baking soda to puff up the candy. It was fun, don't get me wrong . . . but it wasn't dressing up to go see a fancy ballet.

"Well?" Mr. Hine interrupted our conversation. He took out a notepad and tapped his foot impatiently, like he had been waiting there for hours, instead of three seconds. Mrs. Jecknell had somehow convinced him to wear a floppy red Santa hat, but she would have been better off putting him in a Grinch costume.

As the Royals ordered, I studied the menu. I knew my stomach would be rumbling by the time pageant practice ended, but I didn't have enough cash for anything except a hot chocolate.

After Mr. Hine served us, the Royals switched to discussing dates—first up, of course, was deciding the best way for Helen to invite Buddy to the party, but I could feel my mind drifting. Everyone seemed so happy today. And I knew it was selfish of me, but I couldn't help feeling sorry for my-self. I mean, I didn't need luxurious vacations or a stylist to do my hair, and I was happy that Helen already had her date all

47

worked out, but I was starting to feel a bit like a character in a fairy tale—only I knew there would be no fairy godmother coming to rescue me. Or even a regular mother.

As I tried to come up with potential date candidates, I heard Caroline huff, "And we all know Pippa can't do it."

My attention snapped back. I didn't know what the rest of the girls had been talking about, but Caroline's face was all puckered up, like someone had stuffed a lemon in her mouth.

"What do you mean?" Starsie asked, clueless.

"Nothing bad," Caroline said. She flashed me a not-so-apologetic smile, even though I still had no idea what she was talking about. "I know it's just a lunch, but still . . . this isn't a kitchen get-together with a few people. We're inviting other kids, and all of us are bringing dates. It's a special occasion. And let's face it, we have to uphold the Royals' standard. I'm sure Pippa's apartment is cute, but I'm not sure it's up to the cut."

I wasn't sure why they were talking about my apartment, but the tips of my ears were already the color of currants, and my palms had grown sweaty. I didn't think about my response. In fact, I could barely comprehend what I was saying as I was saying it.

"Excuse me?" I demanded. "Speak for yourself. If I wanted to, I could throw an amazing party. You know, Caroline, it's not about the space—it's about how you use it.

That's the secret to the best parties. Everyone knows that."

I paused to take a breath, silently marveling at the words coming out of my mouth. *It's not about the space— it's about how you use it? That's the secret?* I had a feeling I was spouting lines from one of Mina's interior decorating TV shows, but excluding Caroline, the Royals seemed to be buying what I was saying. And I could have stopped there, but since I was already on a roll, I had to add some extra flair.

"In fact, I'm a little sad that I'm not the one who gets to throw the party. I would love to host."

Caroline scrunched up her nose. "It's a nice, *ambitious* offer, Pippa, but—"

"It makes the most sense," Bianca said.

It was times like these that I was glad my jaw was attached so firmly to my face. Otherwise it would have fallen off for sure.

"*What?*" I said, at the same time as Caroline hissed, "B, you can*not* be serious."

"Weren't you listening? I just told you I can't do it," Bianca said.

And that was that. I was never daydreaming again. How much of the conversation had I missed? And what had my big mouth just gotten me into?

"But—" Caroline went into full sulk. "There has to be some way you can—"

"No, there isn't." For once, Bianca directed that regal,

icy glare of hers at Caroline. "I'm serious. There's renovation junk everywhere in my house. My dad would never let me throw a party right now. And it's not like you can do it. Not unless you kick out all seven of your cousins. Helen's parents are having guests over, Win said she can't do it, and there's no way we're letting someone outside of the Royals host. So unless you have something helpful to add, it's settled. Pippa's hosting."

Bianca's voice was level, but frosty. And even though a distant part of me recognized that I had just dug my own grave, I couldn't help but enjoy watching Caroline get chastised for once. She held her head high and aloof, but I could tell by the tense line of her jaw that she was clenching her teeth.

"Fine," she said. She turned to me. "But remember, this is a *Royals'* party, Pippa." She said "Royals'" like I was a kindergartner she was trying to teach how to read. "If you can't handle that, you better let us know now."

My heart pounded all the way up in my ears as I peered down into my untouched hot chocolate, like I could find the solution to this new problem in its murky brown depths.

No way could I afford to throw this party.

No way could I invite all the coolest people at Lakeview to our frumpy little apartment.

No way could I pull off being a real Royal.

I had made a terrible mistake.

As much as my pride resisted, I opened my mouth, prepared to tell the girls that perhaps Caroline was right after all, and we should work out something else.

"Relax, Caroline. She can handle it." Bianca's voice was downright chilly.

Starsie let out a cheer. "Sweet!"

"Thanks for coming through." Win smiled.

Besides Caroline, who was furiously eating her Caesar salad, they were all smiling at me—even Bianca. I felt like a lowly moth being drawn toward their irresistible warmth. I knew I was headed toward danger, but I couldn't turn away from their mesmerizing light.

So instead, I pasted a smile on my face.

"No problem," I said. "No problem at all."

5

MARVEL

23 Days Until Christmas Eve!

Remember, this is a Royals' party, Pippa.

On the bus ride to the church, I kept hearing Caroline's words over and over again. I closed my eyes, focusing on drowning them out, but they fought back, and now they were joined by the taunting image of the Tower card. I could clearly see the flames leaping from the windows.

I'd never thrown a party in my life. And this one had to be one-hundred-percent great. But there was no way I could meet everyone's expectations. Just thinking about failing—which, let's face it, was pretty much guaranteed—filled me with humiliation and dread.

Mrs. Lee's prediction had come true. My world was about to go up in flames.

I stepped off the bus and straightened my shoulders. *Get a grip,* I ordered myself. *This isn't you. It's that ridiculous card. It's filling you with doubt. It's just a party.*

Zipping up my jacket to my chin, I started the two-block walk to the Korean Baptist Church of Victoria. "You can do this," I said aloud, and just as I did, the street lamps flickered to life. I took it as a good sign. I checked the time and switched to a jog. The bus had taken longer than I had expected, and I could already imagine Mina huffing, "You were late on your first day? Pippa, didn't you listen to a word I said? We need Pastor Oh's support!"

But when my phone buzzed against my thigh, I slowed down just a little to check the text.

Thanks again for agreeing to host! Helen wrote. **Sorry that Caroline was so snippy. But the rest of us are all onboard. We love you!!**

As I let out a groan, two more messages popped up.

The first was from Caroline: **Get ready to talk details. This party CANNOT flop.**

My stomach clenched.

I pulled up the next text, this one from Mina. **How many times have I told you to wash out your bowls? The kitchen is a mess.**

My shoulders tensed. It was going to be hard enough to convince Mina to let me have the party, and this wasn't the mood I needed her to be in.

I put my phone back in my pocket and cut through the parking lot. Since it was after sermon hours, the lot was nearly empty, and in the fading light the white stone church

53

looked like an abandoned castle—all blocky towers and darkened windows.

I pulled open the double doors at the front and entered the labyrinth. As a kid, I used to wander through the wide hallways of the church, yanking on locked doors until one of the grumpy old women who volunteered there would scold me. I had felt like a grand explorer back then. I smiled a little, remembering those days. Of course, I had complained almost every Sunday, hating the "nice" (code for *scratchy*) outfits Mina put me in, and mourning all my free time lost to youth group, but still, I did have some fun here, too.

Lost in my thoughts, I turned the corner and headed to the church's auditorium. I didn't hear the footsteps coming toward me until it was too late.

"Oof!"

I bounced backward, yelping. I would have gone sprawling, if not for a pair of hands that grabbed my shoulders. The boy I had slammed into made sure I stopped wobbling before letting me go.

"I'm so sorry," I said, at the exact moment his eyes widened and he said, "Pippa?"

I blinked and took a hard look at him. He was about my age, with shaggy black hair and massive headphones hanging around his neck. There was something familiar about his face—that slightly crooked nose, those playful dark eyes.

My eyes widened. Could it be?

"Marvel?"

My gaze darted from him to another boy standing slightly behind him. Although he was several years younger, he looked just like Marvel. They had to be brothers.

"Let's go," the younger boy said.

"One sec, Peter," Marvel said.

"But we're already late!" Peter grumbled.

"You *are* Pippa, right?" Marvel asked, ignoring him. With a sigh, his younger brother slumped against one of the walls. "I think we were in the same youth group a few years ago." Marvel scratched the back of his head. "Sorry if that sounds a little stalkerish."

"No!" I protested. "I remember you, too."

And I did. It had taken me a second—we had never been friendly, exactly—but now I did remember Marvel Moon. He had been the bane of our youth instructor's life, forever listening to music through his headphones when we were supposed to be watching *Veggie Tales*, and doodling all over his gospel notes.

Marvel looked like he didn't quite believe me, so I added, "You were the one who broke into the supply closet that one time. You swiped those lemon drops we all loved for the classroom."

Marvel's eyes brightened.

"I didn't recognize you at first," I said.

"Probably because we were seven. Understandable."

"And because you had a faux-hawk back then," I said before I could stop myself. I wondered if that was rude, but Marvel just laughed. He ran a hand through his hair, which looked good now.

"You had bangs," he countered. "Really tiny ones that barely reached your eyebrows."

I started to blush, embarrassed, before he added, "They were kinda cute."

I smiled; the blush lingered.

"Marvel!" Peter dragged his hands down his face. He looked anxiously from us to the auditorium door. "We're already ten minutes late for practice! Let's go!"

"Pageant practice?" I looked at Marvel. "You're a part of this, too?"

It made sense—why else would he be here right now?—but from what little I remembered of Marvel, he didn't seem like the kind of person to volunteer his free time helping out in a goofy pageant. But then again, I really hadn't known him very well.

"Come on!" Peter insisted, and the three of us finally made our way into the auditorium.

Because this was the only Korean Baptist church in the immediate area, Pastor Oh had quite a large following. So much so that about six years ago, the parish had raised funds to add this new space to the church. With lines of plush chairs, a huge stage, and big projectors on either side of the room, it was definitely the most modern part of the church. In fact, it was so nice that I doubted even Caroline could find something to make fun of here.

Up on the stage, everyone else had already assembled. As we walked closer, I could see that most of the kids were around eight or nine, although I spotted a few younger ones clustered around Pastor Oh. The room was filled with laughter and noise when we arrived, but when Pastor Oh spotted us weaving through the room, he clapped his hands, and everyone fell silent.

"Ah, we were wondering when you two would arrive," Pastor Oh said, looking at Peter and Marvel. He spotted me and squinted a little. "And is that Pippa? Wonderful. Everyone, warm up, and we'll get started shortly."

As twenty little kids began chanting, "Red leather, yellow leather," in scarily exact unison, Pastor Oh walked down the stairs, meeting us in the orchestra pit.

"Peter, run along and do your vocal exercises with everyone else," Pastor Oh said. "And, Marvel, you make sure nothing is set on fire. Again."

I raised my eyebrows at Marvel, and he mouthed "long story." Grinning, he dashed off to chaperone the kiddos, and Pastor Oh turned to me.

I gulped a little. Although I remembered Pastor Oh as a kind man, that had been back when we went to church regularly. "I'm so sorry I'm late, Pastor Oh. I had to take the bus here, and there was so much traffic, and at one stop this old man had to pay in nickels, which took forever, and then—"

Pastor Oh raised a hand. I shut up.

"Welcome back, Pippa. I'm so glad to have you here," he said, his voice as warm as I remembered. From behind his back, a six-year-old blinked at me. Pastor Oh rested his hand on top of the huge pink bow on her head. "This is my daughter, Annie. It's her first year in the pageant."

If Pastor Oh hadn't introduced her, I would have never guessed the two were related. Pastor Oh was a short, stocky man with a large belly that bounced when he laughed and a long, narrow nose. Annie, on the other hand, was one of those kids who was so adorable even Mina would fuss over her. She had dark hair cut in a bob, amber-colored eyes, and a wide button nose. And although she was less than four feet tall, Annie held out her hand to me like a businesswoman. I reached to shake it; her grasp was surprisingly firm.

"Nice to meet you," I said politely.

"I'm the lead sheep," she announced.

"That's—" I started.

BOOM!

One of the kids tripped and crash-landed in the manger. Artificial hay flew through the air like farm confetti.

There was a guilty pause, and then Marvel shouted down, "I got it under control!"

Pastor Oh sighed.

"It will be good to have another helping hand around here," he said. "I admit things have been a little . . . hectic . . . this year. But now we can divide and conquer. I'll be coaching the angels today, so why don't you and Marvel handle the farm animals? They've been working on the manger scene. The first dress rehearsal isn't until this Friday, so we've just been practicing the lines and staging."

"Sounds good to me," I said.

"Excellent." Pastor Oh grinned. He had been holding an official-looking blue folder, which he now opened. He handed me a thick stack of papers. "That's the script. I have both you and Marvel down as shepherds. That way you can be onstage during the actual performance and make sure everything goes smoothly. Or, at least, as smoothly as possible."

Pastor Oh started to discuss lighting and sound details, but I was still stuck on the last thing he had said.

"Wait, wait, wait," I interjected. "Shepherds?"

"Yes, I think you two will nail the part."

"I didn't know we'd be on stage! Isn't there something else—"

But before I could protest any further, one of the kids

burst into high-pitched wailing, and Pastor Oh hurried over.

"You'll do great!" he called back to me, flashing two giant thumbs-up.

I stared at the back of his billowing robes, my lips turned down in a frown. Mina had told me I was going to help out with the play . . . but she hadn't mentioned anything about being up onstage with a bunch of little kids in costume. What if someone from school saw me?

"Come on!" Annie said, tugging on my sleeve.

I followed her up the stairs to the stage, still frowning. But as we headed toward the chaotic manger scene, I tried to search for a silver lining. After all, it wasn't like any of the Royals would pop up at my church. And although I wasn't looking forward to putting on some rank-smelling old robe, maybe I could turn this into a positive thing . . . I was already doing Mina a significant favor, and after she found out about this next level of embarrassment, maybe she'd actually feel guilty for once and let me throw the party in our apartment without a fight.

"We've been working on this scene for forever," Annie said, cutting into my thoughts. "The other kids keep saying their lines wrong. Not me, though. I study them every day. And over there? That's Hana and Sun-Hee. They're my sheep-kicks. That's like sidekicks, but for sheep."

We reached center stage, and Annie scampered off to sit by her friends. Marvel already had two of the kids sweeping up the hay. When he spotted me, he grabbed a couple of shepherds' walking sticks from the floor and tossed one to me.

He banged his stick on the floor, and all the farm animals fell silent.

"Everyone, this is Pippa," Marvel said. Ten sets of curious eyes turned to me. I gave a little wave. "Under the authority of Pastor Oh, Pippa has been granted the Cane of a True Shepherd," Marvel continued, his voice grave. I had no idea what he was talking about, but it seemed to mean something to the kids. They all nodded seriously. "That means the two of us are in charge. Right, Pippa?"

Marvel looked at me.

"Umm, right?" I said.

Marvel leaned in closer to me. He whispered, "You have to show your authority early, or they'll walk all over you. Trust me. I spent my first rehearsal getting my nails painted with glitter by one of the sheep."

I stifled a laugh, which ended up sounding like some sort of strange burp.

"Oh. Um. Right," I said. "We're in charge."

As Marvel worked with Team Cow and Team Donkey to right the sloppy set pieces, I went over lines with Annie, Sun-Hee, and Hana.

"*Baaawww,*" Annie said. "The Baby Jesus has come. Rejoice, for he is the Son of God! *Baaaawww.*"

Hana and Sun-Hee *baaawww*ed in agreement.

To be honest, I had no idea why the sheep had actual lines, but it was easy enough to sit cross-legged on the floor while the girls argued about whether it should be more of an enthusiastic *"baaaaww!"* or a surprised *"baww!"* After a few minutes, I glanced over at Marvel. The hay was now back in place, but two of the donkeys were playing hide-and-seek. I couldn't tell if Marvel noticed. He had plopped himself down on one of the haystacks. His huge headphones were still draped around his neck, and I spotted a smaller earbud wedged in his left ear. *Some things never change.*

I told the sheep crew to take it from the top and sidled over to him. "You seem to have lost a couple of donkeys."

"They're not lost. We're playing a game. It's called Curtains Up, Curtains Down."

I tilted my head.

"When it's Curtains Up, you say your lines. When it's Curtains Down, you can rest."

"I see. Umm . . . how long have the curtains been down?"

A faint tinge of pink colored Marvel's cheeks. "Five . . . maybe ten minutes?" he said. "No longer than fifteen, I swear."

"Mm-hmm. I'm sure," I said. I didn't know why, but I felt strangely comfortable around him—or, at least, comfortable enough to tease him. Maybe it was because I knew him, sort of. Or maybe it was just that something about him made me want to joke around. "Why are you here, anyway? At the pageant, I mean."

"What, you don't think it's out of the goodness of my heart?" Marvel asked, clasping a hand against his chest.

But when I arched my eyebrow, he admitted, "I lost a bet to one of my brothers. This was the punishment."

Grinning a tiny bit, I pointed at his phone. "So, what are you listening to?"

He patted the haystack, and I sat down next to him, a few inches away. He showed me the screen of his phone: 2YA2YAO! by Super Junior.

"Oh, nice," I said, even though I had never heard the song before. "I like Super Junior."

"What do you think of this one? I've been listening to it nonstop."

I cringed. I had hoped he wouldn't ask me.

"Umm . . . ," I said.

"Don't tell me you've never heard it."

"Well . . . "

"You don't listen to K-pop?"

"No, I do," I said. "Sometimes. I used to listen to it more." And because I sounded like I was lying, I added, "Really." Which probably made it sound like even more of a lie.

But I was telling the truth. I listened to BTS whenever I needed to cheer up, and I still grooved to all my favorites. But mostly, I listened to the songs Mina had been into when she was younger—like "Tell Me," "Hot Issue," and "Day by Day." I listened to Super Junior, too, but I hadn't checked out their new releases in years. Since none of the other kids at Victoria Middle or Lakeview listened to K-pop, it seemed somehow embarrassing, so I hadn't kept up with as many new songs. Now I felt even more embarrassed because I couldn't keep up with Marvel.

But while he made a little *tsk-tsk* sound, his eyes glinted playfully.

"Get ready for some homework then."

Marvel held his hand out. I stared down at his empty palm, wondering what he wanted.

"Your phone."

I handed it over, still confused. It wasn't until he started typing that I saw he was putting his number into my contacts.

Even though the whole interaction was giving me a warm feeling in my chest, I tried to play it cool, like boys asked me for my number all the time. Or, rather, took my phone and put their numbers in it. Truth was, I couldn't remember any time this had happened. Buddy and I hadn't swapped numbers until way after we were friends, and Eliot *had* to give me his number, being my tutor and all.

Eliot. I realized just then that I hadn't thought about him in at least an hour, which—I was kind of ashamed to admit—was almost a personal record. But before I had time to process that, Marvel handed me back my phone.

"I'll send you some of my favorite songs later," Marvel said. "Don't worry. If you don't like them, you can block my number."

"Make sure you pick some good ones, then," I said.

Marvel smiled. He had a nice, kind smile—it stretched across his entire face. In fact, a lot of things about Marvel were nice. . . .

My stomach did a small flip as I realized we were sitting closer to each other than I had thought.

"Hey! That's mine!"

Behind us, Team Donkey and Team Cow broke out into a squabble. So much for Curtains Down. Marvel stood, tapped his cane twice on the ground, then marched over to the kids like a soldier going off to battle.

Wishing we could have kept chatting, I returned to the Sheep Crew. They had given up on their lines and were now playing with one of those little paper fortune-tellers.

"Want to try it?" Annie looked up at me and smiled.

I shook my head. After Mrs. Lee and her horrible tarot cards, I was dead set against fortune-telling of any kind. "We don't have time. Rehearsal is almost over."

Sure enough, within a few minutes, Pastor Oh clapped again, and we all gathered on the edge of the stage.

"Excellent job today!" He beamed. "I'll see you all on

Friday. Tell your parents that you'll be here until eight—it will take a while to get into the costumes."

As Pastor Oh dismissed us, I could see Marvel eying me from across the stage, like he was thinking about coming over. Before he could, Pastor Oh beckoned me his way. I was disappointed that I couldn't talk to Marvel, but I quickly reminded myself that there would be more rehearsals. And then I could feel my forehead creasing, because since when did I want *more* rehearsals?

I headed over to Pastor Oh. "You wanted to see me, Pastor?"

"Just to say thank you for today," he said. "Thank you for running lines with the sheep, uh, I mean, girls! You're quite the natural leader."

I couldn't help the tingle of pride in my chest. Pastor Oh thought I was a natural leader? Me?

"I'll see you next rehearsal," Pastor Oh said. "Tell your family I said hello."

"Will do," I said happily, still glowing from his compliment.

By the time I got outside, Marvel and Peter had already left for home. *Oh well.* I boarded the bus and grabbed a seat in the front. As the bus slid forward, I checked my phone and wrinkled my nose.

Caroline had sent a list of the top caterers in Victoria

to the group chat. I clicked over to the first website she recommended and stifled a gasp. It was *how much* for tomatoes on bread? I blinked hard. Maybe I had read the number wrong. But there was the exact same number of zeroes when I opened my eyes again. I tugged on a loose strand of hair. I had barely thought about what to do for food. Somehow, I figured everyone would just chip in for it. But judging by Caroline's text, I was obviously wrong.

As I panic-scrolled through her other options, Helen texted me.

OH! Forgot to ask. I'm supposed to babysit tomorrow a.m., but Buddy wants to hang out. Can you cover? It's only 3 hrs, so you'll be free by noon! It's a friend of my mom, and she pays $$$.

Although part of me wished Helen had asked me to hang out *with* her and Buddy, as soon as I saw the money signs, I no longer cared. I didn't know how much cash three dollar signs would translate to, but now that I had to pay for the food, I could use as many of them as I could get.

Sure! Just text me the address and I'll be there.

Awesome, Helen texted back. **They're cute kids. Plus, their mom has lots of friends, so if you make a good impression, I'm sure you could get a lot more gigs.**

Suddenly, I wished I was having this conversation in person and not texting. I wanted to hug Helen!

YES! I typed back, unable to hide my enthusiasm. *You're the best.*

By the time I reached my apartment, I was feeling so much better about this party.

With all my new cash, I would have enough money to buy the food and any dress I wanted. Now all I had to do was convince Mina to let me have the party in our apartment. And when she heard all about what a "natural leader" I was, she would have to say yes. I smiled. As long as I worked hard enough, I could do this. I was going to throw the ultimate party *and* wear the perfect dress. Now I just needed a date.

As I headed up the stairs to my apartment, Eliot's blue eyes flickered in my mind. To my surprise, though, they slowly morphed into a pair of playful brown ones. I looked down at Marvel's contact in my phone, and my stomach flipped as an idea hit me.

Who knew? If I played my cards right, maybe I could even have a great date, too.

6

PIPPA PARK, BABYSITTER EXTRAORDINAIRE

22 Days Until Christmas Eve!

"There's our little sleepyhead," Jung-Hwa greeted me. He stood over the hot stove, flipping pancakes. This was something he normally did on Saturdays, but since I didn't have school today and he had a day off from work, it was Pancake Wednesday.

"Morning!" I smiled.

I grabbed three pancakes off a plate, drenched them in syrup, and took a seat next to Mina. She had a full plate in front of her, but she hadn't touched her food. She had her reading glasses on and was focused on sorting through this week's mail.

"So," I said, stuffing a mountain of cakey goodness into my mouth, "I have exciting news."

"Don't talk with your mouth full," Mina said automatically.

I quickly chewed and swallowed. "I'm taking over Helen's babysitting gig today!" I told them, grinning from ear to ear. "I thought about what you said the other day, about things being hard, so I wanted to do my part."

I had expected Mina to look ecstatic, but while she did seem pleasantly surprised, she also seemed concerned. "Are you sure you can handle that? You already have a lot going on with school and the pageant."

"It's just three hours!" I waved her worries away. "Besides, Pastor Oh said I'm a natural leader!"

"Well, I think that sounds like an excellent idea." Jung-Hwa grinned at me.

I smiled back. He looked so proud of me that I knew now was the time to bring up the party.

"Anyways, this is kind of a change in subject . . . but I was sorta thinking that maybe it would be fun if I invited some friends over," I said. "On Christmas Eve. Actually, that afternoon. Like a little get-together. For lunch. I mean, you still haven't met any of my friends," I said to Mina, "and Jung-Hwa loves to cook, so we wouldn't even have to buy that much food, and I would do all the cleaning, and can't you picture how festive it would be? Plus, now that I'm starting to babysit, I can pay for all the decorations. In fact, I'll handle everything! All you two have to do is sit back, have a cup of cocoa, and enjoy the party!"

I finally paused, but only because I had run out of oxygen. I inhaled quickly, trying to restock.

"Also, I think it would help distract us from Omma not coming this year." I felt a little guilty bringing this up— and I really was sad that Omma wasn't coming—but I thought mentioning it could help my cause.

"That sounds great." Jung-Hwa tapped the tip of my nose with his finger.

Bouncing with enthusiasm, I turned to Mina. But she wasn't looking at me anymore. She quietly got up from the table and crossed over to Jung-Hwa. I checked her face for some sign of whether this was going wonderfully or terribly, but I might as well have been talking to the wall.

She handed Jung-Hwa an opened envelope from the mail. And although he was facing away from me as he read it, I could see his shoulders tense.

"You really think it's a good idea?" I asked Jung-Hwa.

He handed the letter back to Mina and turned to me. "I always think you have good ideas," he said, but he seemed distracted.

"Mina, what do you think?" I persisted.

No reply.

"Is everything okay?" I asked.

71

Still no answer.

"Hello?" I waved my arms over my head.

Jung-Hwa nudged Mina, who turned to me. "It's fine. Why don't you go get ready for your babysitting job?" she said. "We'll handle the cleanup today."

I almost did a double take. Mina had accepted the party idea so easily! Not only did she not say no, but she wasn't even making me help clean today!

"Sure," I said. "I can tell you more of the details later. I wonder if I should bake a cake. Jung-Hwa could help!"

Mina and Jung-Hwa had both gone back to ignoring me, but as I headed out of the kitchen, there was a bounce in my step. The conversation had gone better than I had expected. Jung-Hwa was totally into the idea, and Mina hadn't said anything bad—and that had to be a win! Now I just had to nail this whole babysitting thing. Everything else, I was sure, would fall right into place.

I thought about Mrs. Lee's tarot cards and how worried I had been about them. Now they actually seemed silly. Mina was right. The only one responsible for my future was me!

After changing clothes, I headed downstairs and rode my bike to the address Helen had texted me. I showed up five minutes early, determined to make a good impression. I rang the doorbell, then smoothed down my blouse with my hands, making sure there were no wrinkles in it. I had worn the same blouse I usually wore for school, but with a pair of jeans and sneakers. I hoped it would do.

Then the door swung open, and suddenly, I felt a bit overdressed.

"Mrs. Winters?" I asked.

"Oh, hel-loo," Mrs. Winters sang. She stood in the gigantic entryway, wearing a pair of stretchy leggings and a tank top, her chestnut-brown hair up in a messy knot. Behind her, another woman pulled on tennis shoes. "You must be Pippa. And please, none of that 'Missus' stuff. I'm Andrea. This is my friend Maggie. Come on in."

Mrs. Winters—*Andrea*—led me inside. The house was enormous, as most of the homes around this neighborhood were, and looked like it belonged on the cover of an interior design magazine—modern furniture, fresh daisies in crystal vases, and not a single stain to be found on any of the plush wheat-colored rugs. I didn't know how Andrea could keep her house this nice with two kids running around. Mina made sure that Jung-Hwa and I pulled our own weight around the apartment, but it was never this spotless.

"Right this way," Andrea said.

I followed her into the marble-countered kitchen, which smelled like vanilla and sugar. A pan of freshly made gingerbread cookies cooled on top of the stove. Andrea grabbed a list of rules off the table and handed it to me. It was pretty simple. No violent television. Cookies allowed, but no more than two. No letting the sisters roughhouse.

"The girls ate a late breakfast," Andrea told me. "So they shouldn't be that hungry. There's a first aid kit in the bathroom and a list of important numbers on the fridge if anything goes wrong."

"Sounds good," I said.

I didn't have that much experience as a babysitter, but I highly doubted I would need medical help during the next three hours. On second thought . . . I quickly reached out and knocked on a wooden cabinet. Better not jinx it.

Andrea gave me a curious look but didn't mention it. "Thank you so much for helping me out today," she said, sounding genuinely grateful. "I know everyone's busy with the holidays."

"No problem," I said. "I'm happy to."

Which was true . . . as in, I couldn't wait to get paid. But my answer seemed to please both Andrea and Maggie.

"Wow, you're so mature," Maggie said. She grinned at me. "You know, I could use a babysitter, too. . . ."

Automatically, I straightened my shoulders, and brushed my hair back behind my ears—eager to make a good impression on another potential client.

"I could actually use your help tomorrow after

school—I need someone to pick up my kids and stay with them till I get home. Do you have a business card?" she asked.

I shook my head, but as I scratched down my number for her, I was already designing one in my mind: *Pippa Park—A Natural Leader. Just a call away!* Who knew? Maybe I could even get an endorsement from Andrea. I couldn't help smiling. If it was this easy to get another babysitting job, soon I would be booked out. Dollar signs flashed through my mind. I would have enough for the most elegant dress, and a brilliant party, and I could help Mina with the laundromat bills, and I would buy every single sundae off Duo's menu, and—

"And now let me introduce you to Melanie and Eve." Andrea broke through my vision of me throwing twenty-dollar bills into the air. "Girls! Come on down!"

There were footsteps on the stairs, and then a couple of seconds later, Melanie and Eve burst eagerly into the kitchen. They were both grinning—until they saw me.

"Who is *that*?" one of them demanded.

"Where's Helen?" the other asked. She peered around the kitchen, like Helen might be hiding behind the counter.

"Helen had a change of plans," Andrea explained. "That's why we're so lucky to have Pippa here. She can help you decorate Christmas cookies, and I'm sure you three will have a great time. Pippa, this is Melanie, and this is Eve," Andrea said, pointing to each of them.

I tried hard to remember which was which. Helen had told me they were a year apart, but they looked almost identical, down to their lopsided brown ponytails and slightly crooked teeth.

Andrea gave her daughters noisy kisses on their cheeks before quickly saying goodbye. "Yoga starts in ten," she apologized.

"You'll do great." Maggie grinned at me.

And then the two moms were out the door, and I was officially the Adult. I felt a tingle of nerves. It was different at pageant rehearsals—there, Pastor Oh was just a few feet away, ready to take over if chaos erupted. Now it was just me, a seven-year-old, a six-year-old, and the list of emergency numbers on the fridge. My palms started to sweat. Suddenly, I felt a little out of my league . . . and that was before the girls began their barrage of questions.

"What are you going to play with us?" "How old are you?" "Who's your favorite princess? Mine's Belle from *Beauty and the Beast*!" "Will we see Helen again? Is she okay?"

"Whoa, whoa, whoa." I held up my hands. Melanie and Eve looked up at me expectantly, waiting for answers. I tried to remember all their questions. "Whatever you want. Twelve. The Little Mermaid. And yes, she's fine; she just had something else she had to do today."

"The Little Mermaid?" the one who I thought was

Melanie said. "That's my second-favorite princess! I love her hair."

I thought about asking them if they wanted to watch a princess movie—zoning out on the couch seemed like the absolute best form of babysitting—but before I could, Probably Eve clapped her hands.

"Can we decorate the Christmas cookies now?" she asked. "It's a tradition!"

"Umm . . . " It sounded like a potential mess. "Don't you want to do it with your mom?"

"No. We want to do it now," Melanie insisted.

The two girls stared up at me with wide, hopeful eyes—and there was just no way I could say no to them. Not when I needed them to like me. Plus, the cookies did smell pretty good.

Melanie and Eve helped me carry glass jars of Skittles, gumdrops, sprinkles, and peppermints from the massive pantry to the marble island. They had every type of decoration I could think of. In fact, I kind of felt as though we were backstage on a Food Network cooking show. They even had those fancy pastry bags to pipe out icing.

As I hunted for food coloring, Eve and Melanie hovered in the pantry's doorway, going back and forth about what they liked most about Christmas. Now that they weren't glaring at me, they were almost cute.

"Making cookies is the best thing about Christmas," Eve said.

"No, it isn't," Melanie said. "The best thing about Christmas is that school is out, and then Mom stays home and wears those pajamas with the elves on them!"

I tried to imagine Mina in elf-themed pajamas but just couldn't picture it. Even when she dressed up for Halloween parties, Mina always managed to choose the most serious outfits—one year, she had gone as a lawyer; another time, she had dressed as a principal.

I finally found the food coloring wedged behind a bag of chocolate chips and led Melanie and Eve back out into the kitchen. We mixed up colored icing in matching pink bowls, and then I gave each girl their own gingerbread man to decorate.

"Aren't you going to make one?" Eve demanded.

"I prefer just to eat them," I said.

"No way!" Eve said. "Come on, Pippa. Please?"

I don't know why it mattered to her, but I gave in and grabbed a cookie. I was frosting some squiggles around the arm when my phone buzzed, and I covertly navigated to my messages.

At the mall with B if anyone wants to join for lunch! Caroline had texted.

As I watched, a half dozen photos came through. All

of Caroline and Bianca posing in glitzy dresses. **Opinions, anyone?**

"Do we have any more Skittles?" Melanie asked. "I want to add buttons to his shirt!"

"Right here." I slid the jar over to her and opened my feed. Not surprisingly, Caroline's story was full of her and Bianca laughing as they wandered through the holly-filled mall. I snacked on a couple of gumdrops, thinking that Caroline smiled so much more on camera than she ever did in real life.

While I clicked through her snaps, another picture from the mall came in. This one was from one of the clothing stores, which was all decked out with candy canes dangling on invisible wires from the ceiling and gold-frosted poinsettias dotting every flat surface.

Something like this might be cute for the decor. Caroline wrote. **Makes even a tiny space pop!**

I frowned, thinking about the scratched-up ornaments and cheesy snowman cutouts I had found in our decorations box last night. Even before seeing Caroline's message, I had known they weren't exactly up to par. I nibbled on my lower lip, thinking. I might be able to re-create the candy cane effect with some spare string. . . .

"Who do you keep texting, Pippa?" Melanie asked, startling me. "Is that your *boyfriend*?"

No, no, I quickly said—and surprised myself when

Marvel's name popped into my mind. "No," I said again. I checked my phone to see if he had sent me his song recs. Not yet.

"Your girlfriend?" Eve asked.

"No, it's just a . . . friend," I said. If you could call Caroline that.

Eve and Melanie finished decorating their cookies, and I shepherded them into the living room to watch *She-Ra and the Princesses of Power* on TV. As I plopped down onto the ridiculously soft sofa, I peered around the huge room, all the way up to the vaulted ceiling. Crystal snowflakes clung to the top. I wondered how Andrea had managed to get them so high up. Of course, the snowflakes were just details compared to the rest of the Winter Wonderland–themed room. A giant, white-frosted tree covered with delicate gold globes stood in the corner, surrounded by a hoard of red-ribboned boxes. I couldn't know for sure, but I had a feeling that even one of those ornaments was more expensive than our artificial tree at home. Holly wreaths hung over the fireplace, and on the wall, green and red ornaments were arranged into the shape of a funky, abstract tree.

Everything here looked shiny and new, making me think once again of the dingy decorations I had to work with back home. My stomach lurched. This was the kind of place where the Royals should host a party. It was hard for me to admit, but no matter how much money I got from today, it wouldn't be enough to get my apartment looking like this.

"Whoa! Adora has a sword!" Eve gasped. "Pippa, can we have a sword?"

"No swords," I said. "At least, not for a long time."

Melanie started to argue, but before she could, something funny happened on screen, and both she and Eve dissolved into giggles. I remembered being their age. Back then, happiness had felt easy—sneaking candy canes off the tree after dinner or a day spent shivering in the snow, rolling up lopsided snowballs for snowmen. But those days felt like such a long time ago. Back when I didn't have any responsibilities. When had everything gotten so complicated?

Feeling a strange twinge of sadness, I opened up my phone just in time to see Starsie upload a new story—she and Win sat cross-legged on her giant, fluffy pink shag carpet, their faces smeared with green goo. I had never been to Starsie's house—in fact, I had never been to most of the Royals' places—but the fairy lights strung up in the background and the colossal canopy bed both screamed "Starsie." To the picture, she had added one of the longest hashtags I had ever seen: #whenyoutrytostudyanditturnsintoaspaday. It took me a couple of reads just to separate all the words. I couldn't help but wish that I was the third one in that picture, smiling with green goo on my face, too.

I started to put away my phone when another text came through. This time it was Andrea.

Stopped by Stevenson's for lunch. Running a bit late! Can you cover for a little longer? Sorry to ask, but I haven't gotten out of the house for a minute, and we're having such a good time!

No problem, I texted back.

After all, it wasn't like I had anywhere else to be.

I sighed. It might not have been so bad being here, but that was before I thought about all the fun things everyone else was doing. Bianca and Caroline buying out half the mall. Win relaxing with Starsie. And, of course, Helen on her picture-perfect date with Buddy. Everyone was out having fun . . . except me.

I shook my head, trying to shake myself out of it. I didn't want to be with Bianca and Caroline anyway—not when they would just be slinging around their credit cards nonstop, making me feel bad. And I should be happy that things were going so well with Buddy and Helen. Now that they were dating, I didn't have to hang out with them separately—we could all have fun together.

Brightening a little, I sent each of them a text, asking if they wanted to meet up after I finished babysitting.

But no one answered during that episode of She-Ra, and no one answered during the next episode either. Every few minutes, I would swear I could feel my phone vibrating, but when I checked, it was always just my imagination.

"Are you sure you're not texting anyone special?" Melanie asked.

"I'm sure," I said—the saddest answer possible.

For a moment, I thought about Marvel again. He had definitely seemed eager to get my phone number . . . but he still hadn't texted. I leaned my head back against the couch. Despite just meeting—well, re-meeting—Marvel, somehow I already felt comfortable with him. Was he thinking the same thing? Was he thinking about me at all?

Trying not to stress about it, I shoved my phone back into my jeans pocket.

What seemed like hours later, I finally heard a key turning in the front door, and a moment later, Andrea and Maggie walked inside, both giggling.

"There are my little angels," Andrea cooed.

Eve and Melanie rushed into her open arms.

"Momma, momma," Eve said. "We had so much fun with Pippa."

"We decorated cookies, and Pippa said mine looked perfect!" Melanie said.

"I'm glad to hear everything went okay," Andrea told me.

"Yeah, it was great," I said, but my voice sounded hollow even to me.

Andrea reached for her wallet, and I perked up a bit. This was the part of the day I had been most looking forward to. She dug through a thick wad of bills, and finally pulled out a nice crisp one. "Here you go," she said.

She handed it to me. The bill felt stiff and new and smelled like fresh money. And it happened to be a hundred.

"A hundred dollars?" I asked. I didn't mean to sound so surprised.

"I don't have anything smaller." Andrea shrugged. Next to her, Maggie bobbed her head, like this was a normal amount. "And I know I kept you waiting. So keep the change."

Absolutely, positively, *no problem* there. Suddenly, this day didn't seem half bad. A hundred bucks, and it seemed like I'd have at least one other customer in Maggie. And there were still three weeks till the party! At this rate I'd be able to afford food, decorations, *and* my dream dress! Heck, maybe I could even hire a band!

I biked home in a hurry, excited to tell Mina and Jung-Hwa how great my first babysitting job had gone. I knew they would be proud.

But as soon as I rounded the corner of my street, I forgot all about that.

An ambulance with flashing lights sat right in front of my building's front door.

7

NEIGHBORS NO MORE

22 Days Until Christmas Eve (When Disaster Strikes)

I parked my bike in a rush and ran into the building. I stepped into the stairwell and saw two paramedics walk directly out of . . . *my apartment.*

For a moment, my whole body went icy—all the way down to the tips of my fingers.

As I raced up the stairs, all I could think about was Mina and Jung-Hwa. My anxiety surged into overdrive. With each step, a new, horrific image flashed through my mind.

Mina gasping for breath.

Jung-Hwa clutching his chest.

Blood soaking into the carpet . . .

"Mina! Jung-Hwa!" I tore through the open door. *Please let them be okay, please let them be okay. . . .* "What happened? Are you—"

I trailed off at the sight of our apartment.

I had been expecting something straight out of a horror movie, but what I saw was somehow even more baffling. It looked as though, in the time I had been gone, Mina and Jung-Hwa had decided to pack up and move. The two of them shuffled around the kitchen like worker ants. Jung-Hwa carried a stack of blankets and sheets to the living room, while Mina dragged around plastic bins full of clothes. Unfamiliar knick-knacks—paperback books, lotion bottles, a Shake Weight—dotted the kitchen table.

And neither of them said a word when they saw me. It was as if I were invisible. I looked down at my own hands, just to check that I could still see myself. *Definitely there.*

Jung-Hwa headed for the living room, and I darted after him.

"Jung-Hwa, what's—" As I reached the living room, I slid to a stop . . . or, at least, I slid to a stop in what was once our living room. Now it looked completely different. The couch and the coffee table were shoved up against the wall. Smack-dab in the center of the room sat a hospital bed.

And on top of it was Mrs. Lee—perched like a princess, with her left leg in a cast, gingerly resting on one of our couch pillows. As I blinked in surprise, she gave a snort of laughter, staring at the television. I squinted. Was she watching *The Powerpuff Girls*?

"Mrs. Lee?" I asked, bewildered.

"Oh, hello, dear." She twisted her torso toward me. "Have you ever seen this show? It's about three teeny-tiny girls who have superpowers. It's a hoot!"

"What happened?" I demanded, ignoring her question. "Are you okay?"

Before she could respond, Jung-Hwa finally spoke up. "Mrs. Lee had a fall this morning," he explained. "Mina and I found her at the bottom of the stairs. She tripped."

"Over my cat, Boz," Mrs. Lee interjected. "I know he's ashamed of himself. Oh well. It will do him good to reflect on his actions."

"She fractured her tibia," Jung-Hwa said.

"And the fibula! Don't forget the fibula!" Mrs. Lee reminded him. Although it must have hurt, she sounded a little proud, like she was recounting a battle story.

"That's awful," I told her.

"At my age, I could have broken half my body," she told me, even more enthusiastically. "I must still have it."

Only Mrs. Lee could break two bones and look so pleased about it.

But I was still confused. "Why was there an ambulance in front of our building—and two paramedics coming out of this apartment? They don't usually drive people home from the hospital, do they?"

"My friend Harry is an ambulance driver, and he

offered to bring me home," Mrs. Lee explained. "I'm so lucky."

Mina scowled at me and Jung-Hwa. "What are you two doing, standing around? Go bring in the rest of Mrs. Lee's things," she ordered.

She has more things? Already, the living room was cluttered with her stuff. Her phone and laptop were charging in the only two living room outlets; she had a mini-vanity with a mirror set up next to her bed, and I just knew I was going to trip over Boz's litter box on the way to the bathroom late at night. Crates of face creams, spa masks, lipsticks, and moisturizers dotted the floor, and she had her creepy tarot cards set up on the coffee table. I tried not to look at them.

How many more things did she need? And why did she need them in our apartment?

But Mina seemed on the edge of a stress breakdown, so I knew better than to question her right now. Instead, I held the door open as Jung-Hwa dragged in two suitcases from Mrs. Lee's apartment. Before he could go back upstairs for more, I grabbed him by the sleeve.

"Why are we bringing all Mrs. Lee's things down here?" I demanded, keeping my voice low.

"I told you," Jung-Hwa said, his voice gentle. "She broke—"

"Her tibia, and her fibula," I recited. "I know. But did she break her apartment, too?"

"Living by herself on the fifth floor is too hard for

her right now," Jung-Hwa explained. "With no elevator, we thought it would be easier for her if she stayed with us for a bit. Just until she can walk on her own. She'll probably need that cast on for six weeks, at least. But we're hoping she'll be able to manage the stairs after about a month."

A month?

The number didn't sound real. In a month, December would be over. The Royals' party was twenty-two days away. I *needed* our living room back.

"But . . . doesn't she have any friends?"

"Come on, Pippa," Jung-Hwa chided me. "We are her friends."

I wrinkled my nose, about to argue some more, but before I could, Mina peeked her head out from the living room.

"Jung-Hwa! Do you know where Mrs. Lee's jacket is? Could you check her bedroom?"

"On it!" Jung-Hwa said.

"But, Jung-Hwa—" I started.

"I'm sorry. I can't talk right now."

His voice wasn't harsh, but I still felt my throat get tighter. My stomach twisted as I headed back into the living room.

"I like what you've done with the place," Mrs. Lee was telling Mina. "It's nice to get a change. I feel like I won a vacation!" She turned to me and grinned. "We're going to be roommates, Pippa. Isn't that exciting?"

8

ROOMMATES

21 Days Until Christmas Eve

(AKA Why Elevators Should Be a Thing Everywhere)

"A month!" I stood in the kitchen with Mina as she prepared a cup of tea for Mrs. Lee. "Her bed takes up half the living room! What about my party?"

"Pippa."

"And did she have to bring her whole apartment with her? Why does she even need all this?"

"Pippa!" Mina snapped. She ran a weary hand down the side of her face, glaring at me like *I* was the problem. "Will you stop thinking about yourself? Mrs. Lee needs our help. Besides, I don't know what you're talking about. I never said yes to any party!"

My mouth fell open. She never said yes?

"Yes, you did!"

"Mina, dear? How's that tea coming along? I'm positively parched!" Mrs. Lee called out.

"Coming!" Mina replied.

"But—" I said.

I waited for her to tell me that we would talk about this later, but she didn't even look at me. As she fussed over Mrs. Lee, I played back our conversation from the morning, trying to see where it had all gone so wrong.

My phone vibrated against my thigh. It was Helen.

Sorry, didn't see yr txts! Just got done hanging out with Buddy. I didn't notice how much time was passing :D

I also had a new text from Starsie in the Royals' group chat. **Anyone down for Duo's? I can't take any more studying. UGH!**

My fingers hovered above the keyboard. I could really go for an afternoon shake more than ever right now.

"Is Jung-Hwa back yet? I need him to make Mrs. Lee a snack!" Mina called from the living room. "She should eat something. I'll put away the rest of her things. And where is that cat? Pippa, find him! The last thing we need is for Boz to get loose outside."

With a sigh, I pocketed my phone. I didn't text anyone. I knew better than to ask if I could go to Duo's right now.

I headed out to track down Boz, but as soon as I left the apartment, I slumped down on the stairs. I focused on taking deep breaths, attempting to stay calm. I was still trying to process everything that had happened in the last half hour.

My phone buzzed again, and I snatched it from my pocket, ready to turn off the group chat entirely. I didn't want to hear about how much fun everyone was having at Duo's, and I definitely didn't want to deal with Caroline micromanaging my increasingly impossible party.

But this time, it wasn't any of the Royals. Buddy had sent me links to three different enamel pins—one of two cheery looking bumblebees, another of a faux-ruby encrusted Mario, and one more of a crying Casper that said "boo-hoo."

Need your advice. Which one is more Helen's style?

I rolled my eyes. **You're the one dating her . . . ,** I started to text, but then I stopped myself. While it was true, it was also mean. And it wasn't Buddy's fault that I was having a bad day.

I thought about pouring out my heart to him—about Omma, about Mrs. Lee staying in the living room, about how much I missed both him and Helen, and about how it felt like they had chosen each other over me.

I sighed. No, I couldn't say that to Buddy.

I vote bumblebees, I wrote.

I hit Send as something shifted behind me. I looked over my shoulder just in time to see a flash of brown, and then Boz was curled up in my lap.

I scrunched up my face at him. His tail gave a small flick.

"What went wrong, Boz?" I asked. I scratched him behind his ears, and his yellow eyes slowly closed. "Why can't stuff go right for once?"

He gave a contented purr.

"Why do I always feel like I'm on the outside? With my best friends. In my own apartment."

Boz stretched out and turned belly-up in my lap. "Don't get me wrong, I like Mrs. Lee," I told him, scratching the fur on his chest. "I just—ow!"

I jerked my hand back. He had bitten me!

He rolled over and squirmed off my lap, looking offended.

I sighed. Maybe I deserved that. Scooping the cat up in my arms, I headed back inside the apartment. I found Mina and Jung-Hwa in the living room, propping up Mrs. Lee.

"I found Boz," I said.

"That's great!" Mrs. Lee said. "Sometimes it takes me hours. You must be a natural cat wrangler."

"Pippa, we're off to pick up prescriptions and some other things for Mrs. Lee," Mina said. "Keep her company until we get back, okay?" She rummaged through her purse. "Oh, I'm short on cash. Lend me your babysitting money."

"My babysitting money?" My voice reached an octave I'd never heard before.

"I'll give it back to you." Mina's stare felt like a knife penetrating my brain.

"Yes, not to worry, dear," Mrs. Lee piped in. "I'll repay your sister just as soon as I can get to the bank." I knew Mrs. Lee would keep her word, but I still felt anxious. I fished the hundred out of my pocket and handed it to Mina. She looked at me with raised eyebrows, then tucked it into her purse as she and Jung-Hwa headed out the door.

I shook my head, let out a deep sigh, and sat down next to Mrs. Lee.

"Goodness! Things can't be that bad." Mrs. Lee smiled brightly.

My shoulders sagged. That was so not true.

"This, too, shall pass." She leaned over and patted my knee. "Let's do something fun while we wait for Mina and Jung-Hwa to return. Oh, I have an idea." Her eyes lit up. "How about another tarot card reading?"

. . .

Soooooo, about that party? First, let me just say: don't physically harm me, Caroline. . . .

No, that wouldn't work. Think, Pippa!

Attention, everybody. A bolt of lightning struck my apartment, burning the whole building to the ground. Everything is ashes. Rubble. Ruins. And no, you're not allowed to see.

I stared blankly into my locker as I tried to think of the best way to let the Royals know about my new predicament. Last night, I had quickly turned down Mrs. Lee's offer to do another reading, but maybe I shouldn't have. Maybe it would have helped me come up with something to say today. But, really, my only option was to just spit it out . . . and I knew I *had* to do it today. The longer I waited, the harder it would be to tell them.

Of course, once I did, Caroline would make sure the whole school knew about my failure. I'd basically become invisible. No one would want to get caught talking to me. Only losers hung out with losers.

As I grabbed my algebra textbook, my phone buzzed. I winced. The absolute last thing I needed right now was a teacher confiscating my cell. Shielded by my locker door, I peeked at the text.

Hi, Pippa! This is Maggie. Just confirming that we're still on for today! Kids have extracurriculars at school, so you just need to pick them up from there.

For a second, I had to remind myself who Maggie was. With all the Mrs. Lee chaos, I had forgotten. *Right. Babysitting.* I quickly texted, **Got it, will be there**.

Just as I was closing my locker, I spotted Caroline and Bianca walking arm in arm down the hallway toward me.

"Pippa!" Caroline said, her tone already reprimanding. "Didn't you get any of my messages about the party?

Why didn't you answer me?"

"Oh, sorry," I said. "Things on my end were a little hectic." My pulse started to race. Now was my opportunity to fess up.

But just as I was opening my mouth, both Caroline and Bianca glanced behind me. From the way Bianca quickly fixed her hair, I knew exactly who they were looking at. Instinctively, I ran my hands over my skirt to smooth down the wrinkles.

"Hey, Eliot," Caroline said warmly, her chilly tone doing a one-eighty. She waved to him.

I turned just in time to see Eliot walk up. As always, my heartbeat turned to a rapid flutter just looking at him, and I hugged my textbook closer to my chest. It wasn't my fault; it should be illegal for his golden hair to be that perfectly tousled. And those cool blue eyes . . .

"Oh, hey, guys," he said, leaning against the locker next to mine. "What's up?"

"Lots, actually," Caroline said. "You know, it's that time of the year!"

"Um, the holidays?" Eliot asked. "Yeah, I can tell." He gave a pointed look around the hallways, his eyes lingering on the paper snowflakes dotting the walls and the "Season's Greetings" banners on the classroom doors.

"She's talking about the Royals' Christmas party,"

Bianca corrected him. "We threw one last year, remember?"

"And it's a must-show, Eliot," Caroline said, her voice silky but forceful. "Besides, guess who's throwing it this year?" Caroline swung her arm around my shoulder and pulled me closer, like a spider trapping a squirming fly in her web. She smelled like vanilla perfume from Bath & Body Works: cloyingly sweet.

"Pippa?" Eliot asked, surprised.

"Yeah," Bianca said. "I couldn't host, so she volunteered to take my place."

I searched for the scorn in her voice, but she just seemed focused on Eliot.

"We're all so excited to see how it goes," Caroline said, a laugh in her voice. "But you're probably too busy."

I took a deep breath. Time to get it out.

"Actually," Eliot said, "it sounds fun."

My mouth snapped shut.

"It'll be nice to do something different." Eliot turned to me and our eyes met. My stomach was full of fireworks as he said, "Pippa, am I invited?"

Is he invited? A month ago, I would have given away everything I owned just for him to talk to me outside of tutoring. And now he was asking if he could come to my party? I couldn't speak. I could barely stay upright.

Caroline let out a tinkly laugh. "Of course you are!

Like you even have to ask," she cooed, and tapped him playfully on the arm. "You can be Bianca's plus-one."

Eliot blinked. The air rushed out of my lungs. Caroline's smile was triumphant . . . until she caught Bianca's death-glare. Caroline's look could set you on fire, but Bianca's could freeze you, and I had a feeling Caroline was getting a bad case of the shivers right now.

"Thanks," Bianca said in a voice that cut like Jung-Hwa's sharpest cleaver. "But, you know, I am capable of arranging my own date. Just like Pippa is capable of hosting this party."

Her glance moved to Eliot, then to me, and I swear she looked faintly apologetic. "See you all later," she said, and turned to walk away.

Caroline stood a second longer, her face pale and her mouth hanging open. Then she scurried after Bianca. I could hear her speaking in a low tone, but Bianca's only response was to walk a little faster.

"O-kay." Eliot gave me a little shrug as he straightened up. "I better get to class, too. See you for tutoring in the library later, Pippa."

"Right," I said, still trying to figure out what had just happened. I hadn't gotten out of hosting the party—that was bad. But now Eliot was coming—that was good. Very, very good.

Was he coming as Bianca's date? I honestly had no idea.

It was only as Eliot was disappearing around the corner that I remembered Maggie's text. Oh, no. I'd double-booked babysitting and tutoring!

The classical music that Lakeview used instead of bells in between periods stopped. Silence fell in the hall. Uh-oh! I sprinted toward my next class. My mind was going even faster than my legs. I needed the babysitting money if I was going to pull this party off somehow. I needed tutoring if I was going to pass my algebra test next week. (And let's be honest, I needed to spend a little more time staring at Eliot's perfect profile.)

Somehow, I was going to make it all work.

9

EASY (MOSTLY)

21 Days Until Christmas Eve (Eep!)

"Pippa, you lied to us." I looked over at seven-year-old Tara, who was sitting next to me in the library. She gave me a sour-lemon stare and folded her arms.

"This is *not* fun. You lied, Pippa," she repeated.

"Yeah," her younger brother, Alan, agreed. "Coloring is boring. And you don't even have the cool crayons."

"You have all the ones you need. Besides, everyone loves to color!" I insisted. "Now, why don't you finish your pictures?"

My two new babysittees exchanged a mutinous look but went back to work.

Across the table from me, Eliot raised his eyebrows, like he was about to ask if I was *sure* I didn't want to reschedule today's tutoring lesson, but before he could, I quickly cleared my throat.

"So, where were we?" I asked him. "Real numbers? Or fake ones?"

I smiled with all my teeth, trying to convince him as much as the kids that this dual tutoring/babysitting session wasn't just an okay idea—it was a great one. And it was. I had sprinted out of basketball practice as soon as Coach Ahmad blew her whistle and managed to make it to the kids' after-school art class with thirty seconds to spare. And even though keeping five-year-old Alan from running through the stacks was stressful (the librarian had already scolded me twice), I reminded myself that I was sitting in Lakeview's posh library with the cutest boy in school only a foot away from me. And he was looking *extra* cute today. I was trying hard not to stare, but the afternoon light streaming through the library's glass ceiling made the blue of his eyes gleam like a glacier. And the bonus—lots of kids had already seen us together. I could practically feel my social status rocketing.

"All right, so it's important to remember that real numbers include everything from negative numbers to fractions," Eliot said. "So, if you flip to page fifty-three . . ."

Eliot began to ramble about integers, and decimals, and a bunch of other words that sounded much scarier than they were, and I settled back in my chair, trying not to focus on how his eyes lit up even more whenever he talked about math.

"Pippa, how much longer are we going to be here?" Tara groaned.

"Yeah, it's been *years*," Alan added. "We're dying!"

"Oh, come on," I said, sneaking a nervous peek at Eliot. I didn't want him to think the kids were slipping out of my control. "Isn't it *cool* that you get to hang out in the big kids' library? I bet your friends will be super jealous."

"Big whoop," Alan grumbled. "I want to play."

That's when I had a brainstorm. "You *can* play," I declared. "I've got some great games on my phone."

Tara pursed her lips, but I noticed that she looked interested. "My mom says we're only allowed to have an hour of screen time every day."

"For cartoons, sure," I agreed, thinking fast. "But what about educational games? There's *Words with Friends*—"

"Alan can't read," Tara pointed out. "He can't play word games."

"Okay, how about tic-tac-toe?" I suggested, feeling slightly desperate.

"Is that educational?" Eliot asked doubtfully.

I felt a brief urge to shake him by his adorable shoulders. "Is it educational?" I repeated. "Totally! I mean, it's got X in it! That's algebra!" As he opened his mouth again, I rushed on, "And . . . and there's strategy, and . . ."

"Okay." Tara held out her hand, and I gave her my phone. She and Alan bent their heads over the screen.

As I turned back to Eliot, I heard my text alert buzz. Before I could take the phone back from Tara, she read the incoming message aloud. "Caroline says, **'Working on invite list. Royals +1 each + 2 friends each and each friend gets +1. That's 36. Can you handle that?'**"

Thirty-six kids? An image of my living room flashed through my mind. Three on the couch, one in the easy chair, four on our ratty vinyl-covered kitchen chairs . . .

I gulped.

Eliot cocked his head. "You think everyone will fit in your apartment?" he asked.

"Um," I hedged. Half-joking, I said, "I don't suppose you'd want to have the party at your house?"

Eliot let out a single bark of a laugh. "Hah. You've met my great-aunt."

Eliot's great-aunt, Evelyn Haverford, was among the most terrifying old ladies I had ever met. I tried to picture her, in her faded costumes from fifty years ago, mingling with the Royals. "Good point," I admitted.

For a moment, Eliot and I looked at each other, smiling, and I felt a glow of happiness bubble up in my chest. Were we bonding?

"Anyhow." Clearing his throat, Eliot turned back to the math textbook. "I think we have about ten minutes left, so should we look at problem four?"

I pulled my notebook toward me and started writing down the numbers he tossed off, but I still felt that little glow. As he went on and on about something that was most likely extremely important for me to know, all I could focus on was that ridiculously cute crease in his forehead.

"Who's Buddy?" Tara piped up suddenly.

"Huh?" I glanced at her, startled. She was clutching my phone and flicking her finger up the screen as she scrolled. She was reading my texts—again!

"Is he Helen's new boyfriend?" Tara persisted.

"Helen has a boyfriend?" Alan asked.

"I don't think—" I started to say, but Tara interrupted.

"Is that why Helen can never babysit us anymore?" she wanted to know.

"Ewwww! I bet they, like, kiss and stuff." Alan made a gagging noise. "That's gross!"

"I think I'd better take my phone back," I said, but Tara ignored me.

"Do you have a boyfriend?" she asked.

"Yeah, is Eliot your boyfriend?" Alan chimed in. "Is that why you keep staring at him?"

"I do not!" I sputtered, aware that my cheeks were

probably the same color as Alan's bright crimson jacket.

"Yes, you do. I bet you want to kiss him!" Alan pursed his lips and made loud smooching noises.

Tara started snickering. Then she started making kissy noises, too. In no time, the two of them were cracking each other up. "Mwah! Oh, Eliot, I loooove you!"

It was all I could do not to slide under the table. I snuck a glance at Eliot. His face was frozen, and he had this deer-in-the-headlights look I'd never seen on him before.

Then the librarian, Mr. Ortiz, came over to our table. "I'm sorry, but you kids are just too disruptive, and the students here are trying to study," he said. "You need to take it outside."

"But—" I protested.

Mr. Ortiz shook his head. "You already had two warnings," he pointed out. "Next time, try the lower school library. They don't mind a little noise there."

Eliot was already standing up to go. "Sorry," I mumbled. I still couldn't look at him.

"Text me if you want to reschedule," he said and headed for the door.

Mortified, I packed up my books, collected Tara and Alan, and herded them out. "I can't believe you guys did that to me!" I complained. "I'm so embarrassed!"

"But it was fun!" Alan protested. And in fact, when I

got them back to their house, both he and Tara were interrupting each other as they told their mother what a good time
they'd had in the big kids' library—until the mean librarian
kicked them out.

Maggie was smiling as she handed me two twenties.
"I'm amazed that you managed to keep them entertained in
the library for a whole hour," she told me. "Good job!"

Although I was still stressing about the party, and
still embarrassed by the scene with Eliot, my spirits rose as I
tucked those crisp new bills into my pocket. I'd earned almost
a hundred and fifty dollars in two days!

I had just left Maggie's house when a text from Mina
came through.

**_Where are you? Need someone to massage Mrs. Lee's
foot. Her circulation is poor. Come home NOW._**

At the thought of squeezing Mrs. Lee's flaky,
bunion-covered foot, my cheeks turned green. I considered
"not seeing" Mina's message, but I needed to be on her good
side more than ever. Scrambling onto my bike, I pedaled home,
my mind more focused on numbers than the road.

Thirty-six kids. That number went down to thirty-two if I didn't bring two friends and their guests, which was
easy, since outside of Buddy and the rest of the Royals, I didn't
have any other friends to invite anyway. I didn't need to invite
Marvel—he hadn't even texted me. But thirty-two was still a
gigantic number.

I chewed my bottom lip and pedaled faster.

Helen was for sure bringing Buddy, but if I asked her really sweetly and threw in some cherry-flavored Jolly Ranchers (her favorite), maybe I could convince her not to invite the two other people. That would get me down to twenty-eight kids, which sounded at least a little more manageable and would probably bring the food costs down a bit, too.

As for the problem of Mrs. Lee . . . maybe I could decorate her hospital bed like a sleigh and have the guests take "rides" on it? No, scratch that—that was a terrible idea!

I took a deep breath of the crisp, wintry air and told myself to keep positive. I still had time to solve this.

"There you are. Finally!" Mina said as I walked into the apartment. She shoved a sponge into my hand and pulled on her shoes. "I have to run to the pharmacy before it closes. Mrs. Lee needs more pain medicine, and I want to get her some lavender tea. Then I have to go back to the laundromat. Now, after you massage her right foot, make sure to use the sponge to clean around the cast on her left foot. The skin is starting to flake."

With that, Mina rushed out the door, leaving me alone with Mrs. Lee and her crusty feet.

"Hello, Pippa darling!" She waved. "You're my savior!"

Taking a deep breath, I moved toward Mrs. Lee.

My phone buzzed. I swiped to wake it up and read:

Dreams Come True—NCT 127

%% (Eung Eung)—Apink

Dynamite—BTS

Start there and then we'll talk. C u 2morrow.

The text was from Marvel. I was surprised at how much my whole mood brightened when I saw it. I felt a grin spread across my face.

Mrs. Lee wiggled her toes. "Ready, dear?" She waggled her eyebrows at me. "I know it's every girl's dream to massage old-lady feet!"

That actually made me laugh out loud. Mrs. Lee's eyes twinkled.

"What do you say we watch a little of this K-drama I just started?" she suggested, waving the remote control. "It's about a rich young woman who crash-lands in North Korea and is found by a young soldier. Oh, my, he is so handsome!" She leaned toward me. "I have it on good authority they're going to kiss in this episode," she whispered.

"That sounds great," I admitted.

"Very distracting," Mrs. Lee said, waggling her eyebrows again.

The credits rolled and we settled in to watch, me rubbing gently at Mrs. Lee's instep. Despite having no idea how I was going to pull off this party, and despite having Mrs. Lee's foot in my face, I suddenly didn't feel so bad.

BOZ

20 Days Until Christmas Eve

(Wait ... Less than Three Weeks?)

Later that night when I was alone, I queued up Marvel's first song on my phone and bobbed my head to the beat.

What took him so long to send this? Maybe he forgot about me, I thought, but quickly tamped down my doubts. *He was probably super busy this week, that's all. That's why he didn't text me till now.*

But what was he busy with? Did he play any sports? Was he part of any clubs? I didn't even know what school Marvel went to, I realized.

Maybe tomorrow at pageant rehearsal I could fix that. I stood up and headed to my closet. There wouldn't be a lot of time between the end of basketball practice and the start of rehearsal, but now that Marvel had texted me and I knew he was thinking about me, I wanted to look my best.

Knock, knock, knock.

I turned to the door just as Jung-Hwa peeped into my room.

"Are you busy?" he asked. "I want to set up the Nativity scene before Mina gets home. It'll be a nice surprise for her."

"Just a second," I replied. "I need to pick out my outfit for tomorrow."

"All right. Don't be too long, or you'll miss out on all the fun." He smiled. As he closed my door, I turned back to the closet, where I surveyed my limited options with a critical eye. What did you even wear to look cute at a church's pageant rehearsal?

It was too cold for my brown sundress, and I had outgrown the purple top with the rhinestones. Of course, there was always the navy dress I had worn to my Lakeview interview . . . but that was probably too formal. I wanted to look good—but not like I was *trying* to look good. Tapping my chin, I rummaged through the dozen or so tops hanging in my closet and finally decided on a pink-and-lime-striped cotton shirt. I wore it only on special occasions—when I wanted to look like I actually had a personal style.

Carefully, I pulled the shirt off the hanger and stretched it out on my chair next to my best pair of jeans so they would be waiting for me when I got home from school. Then I switched off the music and headed into the living room.

"A little to the left . . . a little more . . . *aigoo*, now you've gone too far left."

Mrs. Lee shook her head critically as Jung-Hwa carefully nudged around ceramic Nativity characters on the coffee table. In the background, *It's a Wonderful Life* played. It was one of Jung-Hwa's favorite movies to watch during the holidays, although I never knew what made it a Christmas movie.

"Mina still not home?" I asked.

"Not yet," Jung-Hwa said.

I sat down cross-legged next to Jung-Hwa and assessed the progress they had made, which wasn't much. They had put up the barn and the manger, along with Mary, Joseph, and the Baby Jesus, but there was still a lot more work left.

I pulled the giant plastic tub of pieces toward me and began taking out everything that remained. There were a swarm of ceramic farm animals, a handful of angels, and the Three Wise Men. And then, near the bottom of the container, were my all-time favorite pieces—because they were us. Me, Mina, and Jung-Hwa.

When I was four, I had begged Jung-Hwa to put me into the manger scene. I desperately wanted to be in the cozy-looking barn with all the farm animals. So Jung-Hwa bought a five-color paint set at the Dollar Store and went to work. In addition to a mini-me, there were a drummer boy Jung-Hwa and an innkeeper Mina. And although the paint was a little chipped, and our faces looked like they were melting into themselves and, as a matter of fact, it was kind of hard to tell that they were us at all—in spite of all those things, they were my absolute favorite Christmas decorations.

I placed the three figurines to the side and scraped together some fake hay from the bottom of the tub. I looked up just in time to see Boz creeping closer. His head was tilted to the side, and his yellow eyes were trained with unsettling intensity on the Pippa figurine.

"Don't even think about it," I warned him.

I grabbed the figurines and hid them close to my side, which was unacceptable to Boz, who immediately revenge-jumped up on the coffee table to knock over Mary and Joseph, his tail twitching with triumph.

"Oh, get over here, you adorable monster," Mrs. Lee commanded.

Boz looked at her with narrowed eyes, but when she made a grab for his tail, he reluctantly leaped into her lap.

I gave him the stink eye before returning to the work at hand.

"I'll put up the angels and the Wise Men," Jung-Hwa told me. "Can you start on the farm animals?"

"Got it," I said.

As I gathered my petting zoo of pieces, I scanned our too-small living room, trying to envision cramming twenty-eight kids in here. I automatically filtered out Mrs.

Lee's bed and her hoard of knickknacks and put our couch back in its proper position. Factoring in the armrests, we could fit six kids on the couch. Then, if we folded the coffee table up against the wall, a dozen more could sit on the rug.

"Six there . . . " I craned my head toward the kitchen, then looked toward the entry hall. "And another three over there . . . "

"Pippa is so dedicated," Mrs. Lee whispered to Jung-Hwa. "Listen to her count all the farm animals—how meticulous!"

"The lambs look perfect." Jung-Hwa smiled at me. "Do you need any help with the others?"

"No, thanks. I'm almost finished," I said, feeling a little guilty. Just then, Boz leaped back onto the table and began batting a goat between his paws. He started to take off with it, but I grabbed him by the scruff of his neck. "Bad!" I said, removing the goat from his pointy teeth as he hissed at me.

"He's just upset because there aren't any cats in the Nativity scene," Mrs. Lee informed me. "You just want to be a part of it all, don't you, Bozzy?"

Trying not to roll my eyes, I replaced the goat and moved on to the camels. I set the first one directly behind the Wise Man with the crown, then picked up the second one. I was moving him into position when Mrs. Lee said, "Why there, dear?"

I blinked. "Um, because the Wise Men ride camels?"

"Oh no!" Mrs. Lee shook her head vigorously. "That's a, what do you call it—not an urban legend—but it's a myth. The Wise Men rode horses! I saw a documentary about it."

"Really?" Jung-Hwa looked doubtful. "Did they even have horses back then?"

"I'm pretty sure they did," I said. "Otherwise how could you have the Four Horsemen of the Apocalypse?"

Jung-Hwa nodded. "Excellent point, my gangaji."

"The documentary was on PBS," Mrs. Lee put in. "So you know it's true."

I tapped my chin as I regarded the scene. "Well, our manger set doesn't have horses, and it seems weird not to give the Wise Men any sort of transportation." After all, Mary and Joseph had a donkey and the angels had wings, which was pretty much the best sort of transportation you could ask for. "I don't want the Wise Men to miss out."

"That's very thoughtful of you, Pippa," Mrs. Lee said. Then her eyes lit up behind her glasses. "I have an idea! Jung-Hwa, would you be a dear and hand me my purse?"

Jung-Hwa obediently passed Mrs. Lee her giant handbag, and she rooted through it for a moment. "No, not that . . . no . . . no . . . aha!"

With a triumphant smile, she held up a miniature pink Cadillac, complete with fins and a white convertible top. "I got it from one of those makeup demonstration parties a couple of weeks ago," she explained. "I just knew it would come in handy!"

"I may not be a history buff, but I am pretty sure that there were no pink Cadillacs at the Nativity," Jung-Hwa pointed out, but he was smiling as he took the little car and positioned it behind the Three Wise Men.

"Oh, but look. It's perfect." Mrs. Lee clasped her hands with pleasure.

And it was, I had to agree. The color of the little pink car somehow just pulled the whole Nativity scene together. I shook my head and smiled. I really loved our manger and these animals and the magic of Christmas, even in the middle of all my problems.

Together, we put the finishing touches on our Nativity scene. The last animal had found its home when Mina came into the apartment, bringing a gust of frosty air with her.

"There you are, *yeobo*." Jung-Hwa stood up to greet her. "Are you hungry?"

"I'm okay," she said. She slipped off her shoes, then glanced past him. "Oh, you put up the Nativity scene! It looks nice. I hope you didn't make Mrs. Lee work hard."

"Only a little." Mrs. Lee smiled. "Pippa did most of it."

Mina gave me an approving look. That made me feel a little warmth in my chest, like there was a miniature wood stove in there, throwing off a cheery orange glow.

"You should eat something," Jung-Hwa told my sister. "It'll keep you strong. Let me slice up some fruit." Without waiting for an answer, he headed to the kitchen, and I followed after him and Mina.

"You were gone a long time. Was the laundromat super busy?" I asked as my sister unzipped her coat and hung her scarf up next to the door.

"Not really," Mina said. "Mainly it was just that one old man who always washes his colors individually. You know the one. He takes forever to transfer them from the washer to the dryer."

"One is better than none," Jung-Hwa said.

He finished slicing up some fresh apples, kiwis, and Korean pears, and set them down on the counter near us. Mina popped a bite of apple into her mouth, her eyes thoughtful.

"Slightly," she agreed. "In any case, sponsoring the church pageant hopefully will bring in new business."

Mina looked over at me and I froze, a chunk of sticky kiwi clutched in my palm, as I waited for her to lecture me about the importance of impressing Pastor Oh. But for once, she didn't attack me.

"Thank you for stepping up to this responsibility with Pastor Oh," she said. "I appreciate it. He called last night and had nothing but good things to say."

She grabbed one more slice of apple from the plate

and stood up with a stretch. "I'm going to take a shower," she told us. "Pippa, don't forget to help Jung-Hwa with the dishes."

As I watched her leave, the warm glow in my chest expanded. Mina hardly ever said thank you to me. This meant she really did appreciate what I was doing. And who knew? Maybe tomorrow I could volunteer extra time for rehearsals. Pastor Oh would be even more grateful for me, and Mina would be so happy that I would have no trouble convincing her to let me have the party.

But as I stood at the sink, watching the dishpan fill with soap bubbles, I couldn't make myself worry about the party. Not tonight.

Tonight, I was finally starting to feel the magic of the season.

. . .

"Pippa! The school bus will be here in twenty minutes!" Mina shouted.

"Coming!" I leaped out of bed.

I'd overslept and had to take a rushed shower. As I soaped up, I thought about the idea I'd had this morning.

What if we just moved Mrs. Lee back to her apartment for that one afternoon?

Jung-Hwa and I could carry her stuff up the night before, or even the morning of the party. Then she could stay there for the afternoon. Mina and Jung-Hwa could keep her company (which would have the added benefit of keeping Mina and her scowls away from my Lakeview friends). I would even help carry Mrs. Lee back down when the party was over, if that's what it took.

It could work!

My stomach rumbled, which made me think about party food. Maybe I could look up some of the dishes Caroline had suggested—I had no idea what caprese salad was; it sounded fancy—and re-create them.

Satisfied with the idea, I grabbed a towel and headed back to my room. I dried off and changed into my Lakeview uniform in record time. Just as I was about to head out the door, I remembered my navy tie. The tip of it stuck out from underneath my pink-and-green T-shirt. I smiled when I saw it. I was looking forward to wearing the shirt tonight—and to seeing Marvel.

As I moved the shirt out of the way, though, I realized it was soaking wet.

Had I dripped on it? I patted my head to see if my hair was still wet. No. Just slightly damp. No way it had soaked the shirt like that. I picked it up, gave it a good, long sniff—and stumbled backward.

"Uck." I coughed. "Boz!"

I turned to the door—and there he was. Staring at me. With the glow of cat vengeance in his eyes.

"You!" I growled.

He darted from the doorway, and I ran after him.

In the living room, the Pussycat Dolls' "Don't Cha" blared from the TV, and Mrs. Lee, from her hospital bed, pumped her arms over her head, as an extremely ripped fitness instructor shouted out instructions over the music. "That's it, keep going, move those hips, get those arms above your head! Feel the burn. Yes, work it!"

Mrs. Lee shouted, "I'm working it, honey!"

In the midst of this, Boz leaped up into the protection of Mrs. Lee's lap. His yellow eyes fixed on me, the tip of his tail twitching mockingly. He totally knew I couldn't get to him there. Conniving cat.

"Oh, look at you, Boz." Mrs. Lee panted, gazing back and forth between me and her furry little monster. She took a swig of water and gave Boz a wet kiss on the head. "Clever cat. You fetched Pippa. Now she won't be late for class! Good boy."

Mrs. Lee smiled at me. Without a word, I spun on my heel, and slunk back into my room. I stared at the soiled shirt for a long moment, wondering how loud I could scream without everyone screaming back at me.

"No screams necessary," I told myself, trying to calm down. I set out an old black sweater for tonight.

This is a small problem. Besides, sometimes dingy looks cool.

I repeated that to myself three more times as I

spritzed some off-brand lemon air freshener around my room, telling myself that it smelled nice and not like lemony cat pee.

Feeling better, I headed to the front door to put on my shoes. As I balanced on one foot, something fuzzy and warm rubbed up against my calf. I stared down at Boz's backside, thinking about the Sour Patch Kids slogan "Sour then sweet." With a sigh, I reached down to scratch behind his ears . . . just as he turned around, peered up at me, and dumped something small and full of teeth marks at my feet.

It was the mini-me from the Nativity scene. Or what was left of me. Since it was missing the head, it was hard to tell.

My mouth flew open, but I quickly snapped it shut. I was so angry I couldn't trust what I'd say.

Boz curled around my other leg and gave a long, loud purr of victory. Across the living room, Mrs. Lee spotted the two of us and clasped her wrinkled hands to her chest.

"Oh, see how Boz loves you?" she said. "How adorable. I have to take a picture!" Before I could protest, she took out her pink phone and snapped a pic of the two of us. "There. Now we'll be able to remember this moment forever, won't we, Boz?"

I'll remember it forever, too, I thought. *No photo necessary.*

"Who would have thought a broken leg could bring

such good luck?" Mrs. Lee went on. "You know, Boz and I are usually alone on Christmas Eve. But now we'll be here!" She grinned so wide I could see her gold molars. "This is going to be our best Christmas ever."

11

HOT AND COLD

20 Days Until Christmas Eve

(Plenty of Time. Right?)

"I smell sweet myrrh," Annie intoned. *"Baaaaw!"*

"And I smell Frankenstein," said Hana, one of the sheepkicks. *"Baaaaaw."*

"You smell *Frankenstein*?" Sun-Hee, the other sheepkick, cut in. "Ewwww!"

"It's supposed to be *frankincense*," Annie said, impatiently tapping her foot. "I smell *frankincense*. Right, Pippa?"

"Um . . . " Technically, I was supposed to be the one correcting the lines, but I had a lot on my mind. Marvel hadn't shown up yet. Was he blowing off rehearsal? Would he quit the pageant right in the middle? I didn't know him well enough to guess, but I did know that I'd be upset if he had decided to ditch the whole thing, because that would mean he'd decided to ditch me, too.

Also, I couldn't stop thinking about Mrs. Lee. She was so happy to be spending Christmas Eve with us. How could I ask her to leave? *It would just be for the afternoon,* I reminded myself.

Still, I was starting to wonder if Boz could read my mind. It seemed like every time I came up with a plan for getting rid of Mrs. Lee, he'd do something awful, like pee on my clothes or eat mini-me. Was he trying to tell me something? Like "Give up, peasant, for I will ruin your life if you make my queen unhappy"?

Maybe we could move Mrs. Lee just a little—put her in my bedroom instead of all the way upstairs. It would mean one less place for guests to hang out, but I'd find a way to lower the number of invitees. I had already decided to give up my own guests. I bit my lip, thinking. I knew Helen would do the same if I asked her. And if Helen did it, I think Win would, too. That would mean six fewer guests and their plus-ones. Twelve total. That could work!

Are you free tomorrow? I texted Helen. **There's something I want to talk about.**

I started to put my phone back in my pocket, but Helen responded.

Sorry, Pips, already made plans with Buddy. He wants me to meet his parents! I do want to catch up with you soon, though.

Really? Me too! I miss you, I started to text back, but before I could hit Send, another message came through.

I have so much to tell you about Buddy! Like, Wednesday we went on this cute basketball date. He kept pretending he was going easy on me, but really I was creaming him the entire time. And afterward we went to Duo's for ice cream!

I deleted my previous message and sent, **Wow! So cute!** instead. I didn't add that, technically, Buddy and I had been doing that same thing every Sunday for years. Or, at least, we used to.

Sorry, I don't mean to be gushy. I just feel so happy, Helen added. I started to respond, but my phone rang. It was Helen.

Wincing, I answered. "Hello?" I whispered, ignoring a glare from Annie. "I can't—"

"I know you're busy," Helen interrupted, "and I'm sorry to bother you, but I just have to vent. In a happy way, I mean. I am so excited for the Christmas party! Last year, I brought a friend, but I've never brought a plus-one who I *like* like!

I can't wait for my friends to get to know Buddy!"

I already know him, I thought. "Have you—" I started to say, but Helen rushed on.

"Oh, so I already asked my friend Jas from youth group and my neighbor Alana, who's homeschooled. I just wanted to make sure I got them early, before they made other plans. This is going to be the best Royals Christmas party of all time!"

"Right," I said, my stomach sinking. Well, there went that idea. I couldn't ask Helen to uninvite her friends.

"Pippa?" Sun-Hee whined. "Annie poked me!"

"You were standing in the wrong place!" Annie complained. Across the room, Pastor Oh looked up. I turned so he wouldn't see the phone pressed against my cheek.

"I really have to—" I began, but Helen interrupted me again.

"Last thing, I promise. Starsie, Caroline, and I finished designing the invitations. I'm meeting up with Caroline before school later this week to fill them out. Do you know which two friends you're inviting?"

"I'm, uh, not sure yet," I hedged.

"Pippa!" Annie's voice was accusing. "Hana said a bad word!" Out of the corner of my eye, I could see Pastor Oh starting toward me and the sheep looking concerned.

"I have to go," I said, and pressed End in the middle of Helen's goodbye. My stomach felt like I had just swallowed a fiery, heaping spoonful of *gochugaru*.

At that moment, Marvel walked in. Pastor Oh spotted him and changed course. "Oh, good, you're here," I heard Pastor Oh say.

Pastor Oh gave Marvel some script changes, then

headed backstage. Marvel sat down on a wooden crate and was immediately surrounded by a handful of adoring kids. I watched him mimic fighting someone off, and as the kids burst into giggles, he glanced over at me. When he saw that I was already staring at him, he gave a sly grin and motioned me over. My mood lifted like a helium balloon.

"Come on, girls," I said. "Let's go practice with the other farm animals."

"Okay, animals! Time to practice with the sheep," Marvel instructed his group. "Go sit in the hay and memorize your lines. We'll be over in a few minutes to rehearse."

As the kids settled in, Marvel stuck his hand out toward me. I gulped. Did he want me to . . . hold it?

My palms started to sweat just as he said, "Can I see your phone again?"

Oh. Of course that's what he wanted. *Of course.*

"Whose number are you going to put in it this time?" I teased, hoping he didn't notice how red my cheeks had turned.

"Nobody's." Marvel laughed. "But my phone is dead, and you *have* to see this new K-pop group. Their dance moves are out of this world." He queued up the video, then climbed down from the crate so that he was sitting next to me on the floor. He hit Play on my phone, and suddenly, I wasn't thinking about my party problems at all anymore. I watched as seven *unfairly* attractive Korean guys dressed in brightly colored business suits shimmied out onto a neon stage. In perfect unison, they jumped up and down, swinging their arms above their heads and stomping their feet to a fast-paced beat as glittery confetti streamed down from the ceiling.

"Cool, right?" Marvel asked.

"I can't stop watching," I agreed. "They must have trained for so long to get it that perfect."

"For months." Marvel nodded. "Although I've been practicing for about . . . thirty minutes . . . and I think I'm close to becoming the eighth member."

"Riiight," I said.

"You don't believe me?" Marvel's eyes twinkled. He jumped up and swiveled his hips from side to side, then back and forth. I burst out laughing. I couldn't remember the last time I had felt so cheerful. So worry-free. I didn't know how to explain it, except that I just *clicked* with Marvel.

At that realization, my stomach gave a slight flip.

It was strange. When I first met Eliot, I hadn't been able to remember my own name. It was like he was a flash of bright light, blocking out everything else. With Marvel, it was different. I still knew who I was, and I didn't forget to breathe when I looked into his eyes. But despite this . . . every time I thought about him, I got a warm, sweet feeling in my chest. If Eliot was a solar eclipse overtaking the sky, Marvel was a pink-tinged sunset casting a rosy glow over the horizon.

Eliot gave me heart-pounding help-I-might-faint thrills. But Marvel gave me wrap-me-in-a-soft-blanket joy. So, which one was true love?

As soon as that thought wormed its way into my mind, I shook my head. Love? Where had that come from? I didn't *love* either of them.

But I definitely liked both of them. A lot. Which was confusing because they were so completely different. And even though I was mostly sure it wasn't love, what *was* it? And was one feeling more real than the other?

"If you thought that song was good, you're going to go wild for this one," Marvel said, unaware of my inner conflict. As he scrolled through my playlist, he glanced over at me and smiled with all his teeth, and I don't know why that of all things did it, but suddenly, I knew I was about to invite Marvel to my party.

He was cute and funny *and* he seemed genuinely into me. I knew that I had a slight tendency to *maybe, occasionally* romanticize the people in my life. I could admit to that. But still, I didn't think I was reading the signs wrong with Marvel, at least according to the magazines stashed under my bed:

He laughed at my jokes.

He made eye contact when we talked.

He looked at me when I wasn't looking at him.

And *he* was the one who had asked *me* for my number.

So I was reasonably sure he wouldn't reject me. But as I cleared my throat, I could still see Eliot's perfect face in the back corner of my mind. I forced myself not to think about him. It had taken him three months just to treat me like a friend. And even though he had started to warm up to me, I still never really knew what he was thinking. Besides, Caroline had already invited him as Bianca's date. (Okay, that sounded super weird, but it was still a complication.)

Now that my mind was made up, I was totally nervous-excited to ask Marvel. I *really* wanted him to be my date. I *really* wanted him to say yes.

I just had to get the words out. Something easier said than done.

"So," I started off casually.

I forced myself to breathe evenly and to ignore how the brown of his eyes was the exact color of warm gingerbread.

"So?" he asked.

"So," I said again. I took a deep breath and wiped my sopping palms on my jeans. *Don't think about it, just do it.* "I totally understand if you can't make it, and there's absolutely no pressure or anything, but well, there's this party I'm throwing on the afternoon of Christmas Eve, and if you aren't doing anything, I was kind of, sort of . . . wondering if you wanted to come. But only if you're not busy."

With that, I forced my lips back together, just in case I accidentally asked him if he was busy for the fourth time.

But despite my bumbling delivery, Marvel didn't look perturbed. In fact, his eyes lit up, and when he smiled at me, I knew he was going to say yes.

Before he could, my phone vibrated in his hand. Marvel glanced down automatically. When he looked back up, his expression seemed distant, and he wouldn't quite meet my gaze.

"I'm not sure," he told me. "I might have family plans."

He handed my phone back, stood up, and walked over to the animals as the sheep started squabbling with each other again. I stared down at the floor, trying to control the sinking feeling in my stomach and the way my eyes suddenly felt watery.

What just happened?

Was it something I did?

"All right, *great* rehearsal everyone. That's day three without any injuries!" Pastor Oh cheered and called everyone to center stage. Marvel power walked over, leaving me alone with my bewildered thoughts. I kept glancing at him, hoping he would look at me, but he kept his eyes trained carefully forward, as if Pastor Oh was giving us lifesaving information instead of one of his usual pep talks. And as soon as Pastor Oh dismissed us, Marvel grabbed Peter and slipped out the door.

I rushed outside, hoping to catch him. No luck—he was gone.

I bit my lip. What changed? It seemed like things were going perfectly and then . . .

Hold on. My phone had buzzed. Had he seen something on it?

I pulled the phone out of my pocket and woke up the screen. There was a new message on it, from Buddy.

As soon as I read it, I knew exactly what had gone wrong.

You know I'm not a sappy person, Park, Buddy had written. **But I can't help it. I'm in love, I'm in love! And you're the reason why.**

12

SHOP OR DROP

18 Days Until Christmas Eve

I'm in love! And you're the reason why.

I stared down at Buddy's text message and let out a long, loud groan.

Now the whole Marvel-weirdness thing made sense. He'd seen the text. Marvel didn't hate me. He just thought I was dating someone else!

I couldn't help feeling a little pleased that he thought I was that popular. And now that I knew what had caused his sour reaction, I could straighten it out at the next rehearsal.

The tension in my shoulders lifted. I pictured Marvel as my date, and I smiled. Once I told him about Buddy, I was sure he'd be happy to come to the party.

. . .

Saturday morning, the second I opened my eyes, I jumped out of bed and headed for the kitchen. I didn't want to miss Jung-Hwa. I had to talk to him about Mrs. Lee.

I had tried to come up with other ideas but getting her out of the apartment was the only solution. Of course, I felt bad about sending her upstairs on Christmas Eve afternoon. But she'd understand, I told myself. She'd *want* me to have my party. Besides, Mina and Jung-Hwa could keep her company. It's not like she'd be alone up there.

I found Mina sitting at the kitchen table, going over her weekly expense reports. "Is Jung-Hwa home?" I asked, pulling a container of whipped cream out of the fridge.

Mina shook her head. "He went in early. He's picking up some extra hours at the factory," she said.

I slid into the seat next to her.

"What do you want?" she asked, without looking up.

Now for mission number two. I lowered my voice a little. "I was just wondering if Mrs. Lee made it to the bank yet."

At this, Mina did look at me. "You know she hasn't left this apartment."

"But you took my money," I reminded her. "For her medicine. Remember?"

"I remember."

"And . . . ?"

Mina sighed. She ran a weary hand through her hair. "Listen. Let me worry about the money." Her voice was quiet but firm. "You just worry about staying on top of your classes. All right?"

Not all right. Not all right at all. I needed the money for party food and decorations. Why did every aspect of this party have to be so difficult? I squared my shoulders, getting ready to argue, but Mina had already turned her attention back to her paperwork.

Gritting my teeth, I took several deep breaths. Trying to stay positive, I opened a packet of hot-cocoa powder and boiled some water. As I mixed the two together in a mug, I told myself that Mina would give me back my money. And I knew she would.

But I didn't have forever. I needed that money now.

I took my hot cocoa and headed back to my room. Halfway there, I glanced over at Mrs. Lee. She was propped up on her bed, as usual, with Boz curled up in her lap. Both of them were watching one of those ridiculously melodramatic Hallmark Christmas movies, and Mrs. Lee was laughing so hard that it sounded more like wailing. In fact, if it weren't for her claps of delight, I would have thought she was crying.

Onscreen, one of the characters slapped another character in the face, making Mrs. Lee howl again. I waited for the sound to die down before approaching her.

"Morning, Mrs. Lee," I said. "How are you feeling? Any better? At all?"

"Oh, you know me. I'm a fighter," Mrs. Lee said, sounding proud of herself. "Scrappy, that's me. My ankle might be healing slowly, but I'm sure it would be healing at a snail's pace for anyone else."

"I bet spending all your time in a new, unfamiliar place can't be helping," I said, trying to make my voice as soft and sweet as I could. From the corner of my eye, I saw Mina poke her head out of the kitchen, but it wasn't until I added, "Are you sure you're not ready to move back home?" that Mina sprang forward and snatched me by my wrist.

"What?" I demanded as she dragged me into her bedroom. "I'm just thinking about Mrs. Lee's health!"

"No, you're not," Mina hissed, closing the door. She crossed her arms and glared at me. "You're being rude and selfish. Not to mention, you're wasting your time. I told you before, Mrs. Lee is going to be here until New Year's. And that's final."

"Fine," I grunted. And even though I had meant to have this conversation with Jung-Hwa, my plans slipped out before I could stop myself. "But can't we move her upstairs just for my party? We can bring her down right after!"

"Pippa!" Mina gave me one of her signature Mina death glares. "I never agreed to that party, no matter what

Jung-Hwa says. And Mrs. Lee is staying here, and the sooner you get that through your head, the better. *Arasseo?*" Mina barked out the last word in Korean so I knew she meant business.

"Okay, okay, okay," I said, before she could get even more annoyed.

Holding my hands up as a sign of peace, I hurried back to my own bedroom, flopped down onto my bed, and stared up at the ceiling. It was so unfair. Mina had said yes to the party. She *had*. And she knew it, too. That was why she'd brought up Jung-Hwa—he must have reminded her of what had happened.

But I knew my sister. If I argued with her now, it would just make her more stubborn.

Why can't just one thing go right?

I had to make this party happen. If I didn't come through, there wouldn't be a Royals' Christmas party, and everyone in school would know it was my fault. Caroline would make sure of it. She'd humiliate me for the rest of my Lakeview life, and the Royals would toss me aside like a used tissue.

I closed my eyes and saw the Tower card, with its flames shooting out the windows. I shook the image from my mind. Things weren't that bad. I had money for food and decorations—if I could get my babysitting cash back from Mrs.

Lee. I had a date—if I could convince Marvel that he'd been mistaken about me and Buddy. And—I pulled out my phone and looked at the calendar—I still had nineteen days to figure out the Mrs. Lee problem. And convince Mina to let me have the party.

Oh, and I still needed a dress. I headed to my closet. Part of me had been hoping that some strange Narnia magic had happened over the last few days and that I would reach into the back and find a glitzy, jaw-dropping dress I hadn't even known was there. But after several minutes of blank staring, I was forced to admit that my seven outfits had not actually multiplied overnight. I *definitely* had nothing to wear to this party.

With that basic fact confirmed, I crossed over to my dresser and pulled open the top drawer. I had been keeping my cash balled up in one of my lucky purple socks—from the same pair I wore the first time I ever won a basketball game—but now I dumped all the cash on my bed. A flurry of ones and fives along with Maggie's now-crumpled twenties tumbled out onto my navy comforter.

Altogether, I had almost seventy dollars. Would that be enough for food, decorations, and a dress if I found one on sale? No, but if Mina gave me the hundred she owed me, then . . . maybe.

With that thought, I took out my phone and sent a quick text to Helen.

Want to go shopping with me tomorrow?

I expected she'd say she was hanging out with Buddy again, but she surprised me.

120%!

A rush of warmth passed from my head to my toes.

Things were starting to look better already.

. . .

The next afternoon, Jung-Hwa dropped me off at the mall. Helen said she would meet me at the entrance, but now that people were Christmas shopping in full force, it was like playing Where's Waldo? in real time. I wandered in through the front door and immediately started to sweat from the sheer number of bodies packed in around me.

"Pips!" Helen waved. She stood by a cluster of vending machines. At the sight of her smiling face, relief washed over me. I ran to her side, and she pulled me into a hug. Filled with happiness, I squeezed her back. It felt like months since I had last hung out with her outside of Lakeview, just the two of us. I almost felt like busting out one of Marvel's corny dance moves.

"I missed you," I said as she steered us through the crowds.

"Same." Helen squeezed my hand. "I'm so glad you texted me! Buddy had a last-minute family thing, so I was just going to be hanging around my house."

"Oh," I said, letting the syllable hang there.

Of course Buddy had a family thing. How else could the two of them be separated for this long?

As soon as the sour thought passed through my mind, I shoved it back into a corner. It didn't matter why Helen was hanging out with me—it only mattered that she was. We started laughing and gossiping like we always did. We bought a cup filled with mini cookies from the food court and snacked on them as we wandered from store to store, trying on bedazzled skirts and flowy dresses.

"These outfits are cute but not party-worthy. I think it's time for my secret weapon." Helen waggled her eyebrows at me.

She led me to a small shop tucked behind the food court—it was in such a tiny, discreet location that I had never noticed it before. The window display was not very exciting— just a mannequin in a dress that looked like something Mina might wear.

"None of the other Royals shop here," Helen confided to me. "But they have real treasures. Just between you and me."

My heart fluttered with excitement. *This,* I thought, was what being best friends was supposed to be—

eating cookies warm from the oven while shopping at secret stores no one else knew about.

"Come on." Helen grabbed my hand and tugged me into the boutique.

Immediately, I knew why she loved it so much. Unlike the window display, the clothes all looked like they came right out of *Teen Vogue*, and the whole place smelled absolutely incredible. Like fresh freesia with a hint of vanilla. Curious, I glanced at the price tag on a striped jumpsuit close to me—and swallowed a gasp. One fifty? Like one *hundred* and fifty? *Dollars?*

"What do you think about this?" Helen asked, holding up a buttercup-yellow dress.

"I love the color!" I said enthusiastically, trying not to think about the fact that I probably couldn't afford the *socks* from this store. "And the tiny bows on the side are so cute."

"Aren't they?" Helen beamed. "Although it's not very Christmassy. Still, I might as well try it on. If you look good enough, do you *really* have to be on theme?" She headed off to the dressing rooms.

I didn't expect to find anything in my price range, but I still searched the store—and found a discount rack hidden in the very back. I ran my hand across the soft fabrics, marveling that even the dresses that were on sale here were gorgeous. I drifted through a haze of pink silk and emerald wool, until I spotted . . . It.

The prettiest dress I had ever seen.

Sparkly silver with spaghetti straps, it all but glowed in the subtle lighting of the store. I grabbed it before I could stop myself. And the moment I felt the fabric, I swooned. It was smooth and glossy and felt like water slipping over my hands. There was only one left on the rack . . . and it was exactly my size. It was fate. It had to be.

Without looking at the price tag, I hurried inside one of the fitting rooms. I slipped it over my head, then paused—I didn't want to look in the mirror. Not yet. I was afraid that what I saw wouldn't match up with the idealized image I had in my mind.

"Pips? You in there?" Helen called. "Come out and let me see!"

"One second!"

Straightening my shoulders, I looked into the mirror . . . and gasped.

I was beautiful!

I couldn't remember the last time that I had thought of myself as beautiful. Don't get me wrong—I didn't think I was ugly. Just . . . sort of cute, maybe, or sporty-chic. Average. But here, wrapped in silver flecks that reflected gleams of light every which way, with my thick, dark hair tumbling down my shoulders, I couldn't stop staring at myself.

In my fantasy, I would fling a wad of bills at the cash register and walk out into the streets without changing. Of course, Marvel would just happen to be passing by, and he would just happen to see me all dressed up, looking like I had just walked off a Parisian runway. "Oh, hi, Marvel! Fancy running into you," I would say. "Have you met my friend Helen? She's dating my friend Buddy. You know, the guy who sent me that text message Friday . . . "

That was my fantasy.

In reality, I looked at the price tag and just about choked on my own spit. Ninety-nine dollars. More cash than I had today. Even with the babysitting money I had earned so far, it would leave me practically nothing for food or decorations for the party.

Still . . . I had eighteen days, counting today, to earn more. I made a mental note to text Maggie and Andrea later and tell them I was available.

"What do you think?" I stepped out of the dressing room and did a small spin for Helen.

"What do I think?" she repeated, her eyebrows raised. "I think you look amazing!"

"You do?"

"Times a thousand. Seriously, Pippa, you *need* to get this dress. It was made for you. The universe wants—no, the universe *demands*—that you get this."

"I don't know," I said, but Helen's enthusiasm was infectious. "Maybe I'll come back for it . . . "

"Come on, Pips, you *have* to buy it now," Helen urged me. "It might not be here later!"

"You think so?" I nibbled on my lip.

"There's only one left," she pointed out. "And the party is coming up. Who knows if you'll find something else this cute?"

She had a point . . . but . . . I pulled out my wallet and grimaced.

"Oh, if you didn't bring enough cash, don't worry about it," Helen said, waving her hand through the air. "Just put it on my credit card and pay me back later."

I looked from the dress to Helen, then back to the dress, hesitating. *I probably shouldn't borrow money that I don't have,* I thought. Mina was always telling me that.

Only . . . once Mina did pay me back, I'd have more than enough to pay Helen. And babysitting was going so smoothly that I was sure I could make enough to afford party decorations and food in the next two weeks. And Mina *would* say yes to me hosting. I'd find a way to win her over.

With a burst of determination, I hugged the glittery silver fantasy to my chest.

Dream party dress? Check.

13

ALWAYS HAVE A
BACK-UP PLAN

14 Days Until Christmas Eve (What, Me Worry?)

"Keep your breath even, and get those shoulders straight, girls! I want your opponents quaking in their high-tops. Nice pass, Pelroy. Park, I know you can go faster than that!"

As Coach Ahmad barked directions at us, I forced myself to sprint as hard as I could, then even harder than that. The muscles in my thighs felt like overcooked noodles and sweat blurred my vision, but I didn't care. We were in the middle of practice, and although my team was down two points, we still had thirty seconds on the clock—that meant it wasn't over yet.

Up ahead, Bianca sprinted toward the basket, but two of our opponents caged her in. She scooped up the ball defensively, her eyes darting from side to side.

"Over here!" I yelled, from the three-point line.

If Bianca passed the ball to me now, I would have just enough time to go in for a layup and tie the game. She pivoted and threw the ball my way—right as Caroline rushed forward.

I dribbled a step back, but Caroline stalked closer, not letting me get any space. She held her arms above her head, her hips shifting as she tried to predict my movements. I paused, dribbling the ball close to the ground with one hand and fending Caroline off with my other arm. Left, right, or pass?

"Don't bother trying." Caroline's lips curled up into a confident grin. She was faster than me—it would be hard to get past her.

I sneaked a glance at the scoreboard and narrowed my eyes. We had three seconds left. Even if I managed to get around Caroline, the timer would go off before I had the chance to make a layup. There was no way my original plan would work. But that's why plan B's existed.

I took another step back, and then, before Caroline realized what I was doing, I grabbed the basketball in both hands, jumped, and took the shot. Everyone went silent as we watched the ball arc through the air—then swish through the hoop. I didn't even realize my hands were balled into fists until that moment.

Starsie whooped, and Bianca came over to high-five me. "Great play," she said. For once her smile was totally friendly. "I had a feeling you'd go for that shot, and I knew you'd make it."

Her praise and my own adrenaline felt fantastic, and the cherry on top was Caroline's disgruntled expression.

"Good game," I told her, and watched her struggle not to scowl.

But before she could say anything, Coach Ahmad released us to the locker room. I jogged over to get changed. I had a tutoring session with Eliot—at his house this time—and I didn't want to be late. My test was the next day, and after last week's tutoring fiasco, I needed all the help I could get. I'd seen him once or twice at school, and he'd acted normal toward me—as in he'd nodded slightly and not acted like I was invisible—so I was hoping he'd forgotten about Alan and Tara and their teasing.

Just as I was buttoning my Lakeview blazer, Caroline sidled over. Her gaze was vengeful, and she eyed me like she was searching for weaknesses.

"Hey, Caroline," I said, trying to keep my voice cool as I stuffed my things into my backpack. "What's up?"

"Oh, I was just wondering how things are coming along with the party," she said, her voice silky. "You're keeping on top of everything, right?"

"Right," I confirmed, crossing my fingers as I adjusted a strap.

"That's good," Caroline told me. "Because, as I'm sure you know, the clock is ticking down ... "

As if I needed the reminder.

"Caroline, chill." Win glanced our way. "You're making it sound so ominous."

"Yeah." Helen crossed over to us and gave my shoulder a reassuring squeeze. "Besides, there's no reason to worry. Pippa already told you—everything is going fine!"

Helen and Win smiled at me, while Caroline's expression turned rancid.

"I'll take your word for it," she muttered. She flipped her hair over one shoulder. "Anyway, I'll text everyone my final suggestions for food." She turned to me and added, "You might not be familiar with any of these restaurants, Pippa, but trust me—they're fabulous. Two of them have a Michelin star, and the head chef of Fresh trained for seven years in Paris."

"Sounds great," I lied.

I knew I couldn't afford Michelin-starred *anything*, whatever that meant, but food was way down on my list of worries right now. I zipped up my backpack and was about to head out when Caroline grabbed my wrist.

"Before you go, take these." She handed me a thick

stack of envelopes. "They're the invitations. Use the top three to invite your guests. Then write your address on all of them where it says *place*," she said, as if I'd never seen a party invitation before. "Then mail them." She gave me one of her sickly sweet smiles. "I can't *wait* to meet your friends."

I turned away, wishing I had friends to invite . . .

That made me think of Buddy, and my stomach got that sinking feeling. I hadn't actually hung out with Buddy in weeks. I'd invited him over for Jung-Hwa's *kimchi-jjigae* last week, because that was his favorite of Jung-Hwa's dishes. He hadn't even answered me until a day later. Then he apologized for missing my text. His excuse? His mom took his phone away because he was spending too much time talking to Helen.

Buddy used to be my closest friend—but I felt like I was losing him. That he didn't need me anymore now that he had upgraded to Helen. Of course, part of me knew that wasn't true, but still . . .

. . .

I took out one of the invitations. Starsie, Caroline, and Helen had done an amazing job designing them. The card stock they had picked out was the same shade of gold as the scrunchies the Royals wore, and they were decorated with festive red holly berries and a green border. Even the envelope

148

paper was luxurious—thick and glossy. The knot in my stomach grew a little tighter.

I slipped the invitations into the front pocket of my
backpack and zipped it up. At the bike rack, I unlocked my
dinged-up old bike and climbed on, bracing myself for the
freezing ride to Eliot's.

So far I made very little headway with my party problems. Neither Andrea nor Maggie needed any babysitting this
week, and Andrea said they were was leaving Friday to visit
family in Minnesota. So I couldn't count on solving my cash
problem that way.

An icy wind blew leaves and grit into my eyes. I put
my head down and pedaled faster, trying not to feel too sorry
for myself.

I hadn't gotten anywhere with Mina, either—mainly
because it was impossible to talk to her alone with Mrs. Lee
in our living room. Plus, she'd seemed extra tense lately; she
spent most of her free time sitting at the kitchen table with
her head bent over a stack of papers, punching in numbers,
using the calculator on her phone.

By the time I reached Eliot's big, gloomy old house,
I couldn't feel my ears or my fingers or my toes anymore.
Bouncing on the soles of my feet, I rapped on his door until he
swung it open.

"Oh, hey, Pippa," he said. "You were knocking so hard,

I thought someone was having an emergency."

"No fatal accidents. I'm just freezing. And happy to be here!" I added quickly.

Eliot gave me one of his rare grins. "I knew you'd eventually warm up to irrational numbers."

A joke! He made a joke! My insides melted a little.

He held the door open for me, and the two of us walked into the entry hall and through his ornate living room.

Although Eliot's house was richly decorated, with paintings in gilded frames; massive, carved dark wood furniture; and velvet drapes, I had to admit—the place could use some festive cheer. And a good dusting—the headmaster evidently wasn't much for housekeeping. Cobwebs drooped from the crystal chandelier in the dining room. More than that, though, there was a feeling that time had stopped ages ago. My little apartment might be shabby, but it didn't feel *gloomy* like this place.

"So when is your test again?" Eliot asked as we sat down at the long dining table.

I winced. "Um . . . tomorrow."

Eliot shot me a look of disbelief. "Then we should probably do a review of the main concepts. Let's start on page forty-one . . . "

Eliot began summarizing the most important points from each chapter, and I scribbled down notes and tried hard to pay attention. But focus seemed impossibly out of reach.

Not only was there the usual distraction of Eliot—he had clearly come from his own basketball practice, and his cheeks were still faintly flushed from all the running around, plus his hair was damp and his shampoo had a piney scent, which was mildly hypnotizing—but I also couldn't stop stressing about the party, and holding it in took all my limited control.

Focus, Pippa. And stop sniffing him. He'll notice.

"Why don't you try problem number three?" Eliot asked, handing me a piece of notebook paper. "That's the one we were practicing last time."

I looked down at the string of unrelated numbers and letters and resisted the urge to snap my pencil in half. Why was math so *hard*? Every time Eliot explained a problem, it seemed so simple. But as soon as I tried it myself, the numbers morphed and squiggled around the page until I was looking at nonsense.

I tapped my pencil against my thigh, trying to get started with step number one. But now that I was taking so long, I could feel Eliot watching me, and that just made my thoughts more jumbled. I didn't want him to think I couldn't do it.

"Do you need help?" Eliot asked after a long minute had passed.

"No" I said automatically. And then, because it was obvious that I did, I caved. "Actually, yes. I thought I understood, but I don't. I'm sorry." I sighed. "I feel so dumb."

Eliot was quiet for a moment. "Just because math doesn't come naturally to you doesn't mean you're dumb," he said at last.

I peeked up at him. "It doesn't?"

"No. Besides, I don't know why everyone puts such an emphasis on being a genius over everything else. Especially when there are so many other excellent traits and skills to have. Like being kind. Or being brave. Or missing only one free throw this entire season."

My eyebrows shot up so high they nearly touched my hairline, and I stared at Eliot. This was by far the nicest thing he'd ever said to me.

My body tingled as I realized something else: He apparently paid enough attention to me to know I had missed only one free throw.

Was it possible that Eliot actually, truly liked me?

"Eliot!" The imperious voice made me jump. I twisted around to see that Eliot's great-aunt, Miss Haverford, had entered the room. As usual, she wore an outfit that had no doubt been extremely fashionable fifty years earlier—a skirt suit made out of some heavy, dark fabric that looked as if it had been clawed by a gang of cats. Her hair perched on top of her head in a white, wispy poof.

She glared at me down her long nose. "What is . . . she doing here?" she demanded of Eliot.

I gulped. I hadn't been in the Haverford house since before Thanksgiving—and the last time I was here I'd done something a little wild, trying to help Eliot's brother, Matthew. It had all worked out okay in the end, but apparently Miss Haverford had not forgiven me.

Eliot's voice was wooden as he said, "You remember Pippa, Aunt Evelyn. I'm tutoring her in math."

Miss Haverford sniffed. "Oh, yes. Well, service to the community is a Haverford value," she intoned.

Service to the community? Was that why Eliot tutored me? Was I "the community"?

"Tell me, what subject are you focusing on?" Miss Haverford asked me.

I cleared my throat. "Uh—we're working on slopes right now," I said cautiously.

"I see," Miss Haverford said as if she didn't believe me. She turned her gaze back to Eliot and tapped a long, yellowed fingernail on a heavy brooch pinned to her jacket. *Click, click.*

She stood a moment longer, then swept past us and down the hall. Her heels tap-tapped away into the distance.

When I looked back at Eliot, he was staring down at my textbook. "Okay, let's try this again," he said. "If you want to find the slope of a line that passes through these points—" he pointed to a spot on a graph in the book—"and these points"— he pointed to another spot—"what would you do?"

"Ummm . . ." I squinted at the page. "Climb it and see how out of breath I get?"

It was a bad joke, but even so, I thought I might get a smile. But Eliot's blank look reminded me of how he used to be back when he first started tutoring me. Completely stony. My heart sank, and the light, airy feeling I'd had moments ago evaporated completely.

I wasn't sure if it was Miss Haverford who had changed the vibe, or if I'd just been imagining it before. But suddenly I felt as empty and cold as if I were still outside Eliot's front door.

. . .

Outcast. *THUD.* Reject. *THUD.*

Each time I dribbled the basketball, another description popped into my mind.

Inept. *THUD.* Incompetent. *THUD.* Useless.

It was three days later, and I had made zero progress on my party plans.

I took another shot. *DOINK!* The ball hit the rim of the hoop and plunked down onto the cold asphalt of the basketball court. It bounced limply before rolling to a sad stop.

"Ugh." As I jogged over to retrieve the ball, a shiver shook my body, and I zipped my jacket all the way up to my chin. December in New England was *bitter.*

Rubbing my throbbing red hands together for warmth, I centered myself back on the free-throw line. My breath came out in ghostly white wisps as I stared up at the hoop, but although part of me wanted to be home drinking spiced tea with Jung-Hwa, the rest of me wanted—no, *needed*—to be here. On the basketball court, shooting hoops the way Buddy and I used to.

Of course, Buddy hadn't responded to my text telling him I was coming here. So here I was, by myself, hoping the court would work its magic. Usually, I found complete peace when I was on the basketball court. My breathing became deep and even, my muscles relaxed, and each shot felt natural—like I was home. Today, though, that harmony seemed out of reach.

I'd tried everything I could think of to make this party happen. I'd even called around to a few party-rental spaces, but they were all booked for the afternoon of Christmas Eve. Not that I had the money for a party space, but I was desperate.

On top of that, I was starting to get kind of freaked out by my sister. Mina seemed so tense these days. Could business at the Lucky Laundromat really be that bad?

Maybe I should just give up the party planning now, throw myself on the Royals' mercy, and offer all my babysitting money to Mina. Yes, it would destroy my social life at least until high school, but it hurt my heart to watch Mina sitting with her calculator night after night.

Even if I did that, though, how much could I really help? I had only seventy dollars to my name (or negative twenty-nine, if you counted the money I owed Helen). I had a feeling babysitting cash wasn't going to be enough to save us.

There was one bright spot. Today Mrs. Rogers gave back our algebra tests and, believe it or not, I had gotten a decent grade. Actually, the B- might count as a Christmas miracle. But thinking about that reminded me of how Eliot had turned chilly toward me again. I sighed. My spirit felt as gray as the leaden winter sky.

I shook my head, straightened my spine, and took another shot. The ball curved around the hoop before unenthusiastically plopping inside. I frowned. Technically, it counted, but I wasn't satisfied.

I headed over to the benches and slumped down onto the freezing wood. I took out my phone and brought up Helen's number. I didn't want her to know what a failure I was, but I needed to tell someone that the party was in jeopardy. The longer I waited, the worse it would be. I had no choice.

You free? I texted. **Need some advice.**

I waited for a minute, but there was no response.

I looked up at the darkening sky. Soon it would be even colder than it was already. Since being on the court wasn't exactly doing me any favors, I started dribbling my basketball toward home. As I passed through the downtown area, I peered into Duo's Diner. It looked warm and cozy inside and was packed with smiling people.

I slowed down, remembering the first time Buddy had met the Royals—it had been here, at Duo's, and I had been so obsessed with impressing the Royals that I had pretended I barely knew him. I was so focused on becoming one of them, I pretty much stopped hanging out with him. I still felt a heated flash of shame when I thought about how I'd treated my oldest friend. How could I resent Buddy for ignoring me now, when I had done the exact same thing to him?

But that's why Buddy should know better, a bitter voice in my head insisted. *He knows exactly how it feels to be abandoned.*

I needed to go home and drown my sorrows in hot cocoa. As I jogged up the front steps to my apartment building, my phone buzzed. I saw Helen's number—finally!—and my resentment started to thaw.

See? Helen and Buddy are your best friends. Of course they still care about you. They'll always be there for you.

My whole body suddenly felt warmer. I could feel the muscles in my face soften and my lips turned up in a smile—until I read her message.

Sorry, Pips. Just saw your text. Hanging out with Buddy right now. I can try to call you later if he doesn't stay too late.

Don't worry about it, I wrote back glumly.

A second later my phone buzzed again.

I'll tell him you said hi. By the way, I need to give my parents $$$ for my credit card bill. Can you bring the money for your dress to school tomorrow? It was $106 with tax.

I groaned out loud. Wonderful. I was down to negative *thirty-six* dollars, with no party place, no money for food, and no money for decorations. And my sister's business was about to go under. Plus, I was going to be shunned by the Royals and probably the whole school once Caroline got through with me.

And I had no one to help me figure any of this out.

Mrs. Lee's tarot cards had predicted this whole disaster. If I had taken them seriously, would I have volunteered to host the party?

It's too late to wonder about that now. I let out a long sigh. Then I entered the apartment.

Neither Mina nor Jung-Hwa was home—Thursday was a late night at the laundromat, and I knew Jung-Hwa had gone to the urgent-care dentist for a broken tooth. The only person in our apartment was Mrs. Lee. She was propped up in her usual position in her hospital bed, reading a paperback book with a very buff man with long, flowing brown hair on the cover.

Mrs. Lee. Could I talk to her about my problems? After all, they were kind of—in fact, mostly—her fault. If she hadn't moved into our living room, I'd have a space for our party. And if she hadn't needed all her prescriptions, I'd still have the one hundred dollars Mina had borrowed from me.

But although that was technically true, I still felt horribly guilty as I crossed into the living room. I knew Mina would think it was beyond rude to ask Mrs. Lee for the money while she was still recovering. And honestly, I agreed with Mina. But I couldn't see any other way. So I forced myself to stop thinking about what Mina would say if she knew what I was about to do . . .

14

UNRAVELING

That Night and Still 14 Days Until Christmas Eve

"Oh! Back so soon, dearie?" Mrs. Lee blinked up at me from behind her huge tortoiseshell-frame glasses. "I thought you were meeting a friend."

I shook my head. "I was playing a little basketball by myself."

Mrs. Lee set down the book and clapped her hands together. "Well, I'm glad you're here with me. Since Mina and Jung-Hwa are both out of the house, why don't you make a bowl of buttered popcorn, and we can watch that marvelous K-drama together. What's it called? The one with that pretty little thing—*Park So-dam*!"

"*Record of Youth*?"

"That's the one," Mrs. Lee said triumphantly. "I've only watched the first episode, but I'm loving it."

"I like it, too," I said. For a minute, I was tempted.

There was something so comforting about watching Mrs. Lee's shows with her . . .

But then I shook my head. *Eyes on the prize, Park.* "Maybe later. There's, uh, actually something I kind of wanted to talk to you about."

"Oh, girl talk!" Mrs. Lee clapped so enthusiastically that I took a step back. She leaned forward. "I *love* girl talk."

"Well, it's not exactly girl talk . . . "

Mrs. Lee waved a hand. "Girl talk, boy talk, it's all about connecting. I give excellent advice," she told me. "In another life, I would have been one of those advice columnists you see in the newspaper. *Ask Min-seo*—kind of has a ring to it, doesn't it?"

"Mmm." I nodded politely. "But I actually wanted to—"

"Here, sit," Mrs. Lee demanded, patting the empty space on her mattress. "Tell me everything. Is it about your grades? Do you want me to forge a signature for your report card?"

"What? No." I shook my head.

"Have you started your period? You need me to teach you how to use a tampon?"

I shook my head even harder, feeling my ears turn red.

"Boy trouble, then?"

I hesitated for a moment, and that was all Mrs. Lee needed to swoop in.

"I knew it!" she said. "Trust me—there are many things that will put you through the wringer in life, but not many of them are more painful than men. In fact, that's how I ended up here."

"In our living room?" I blurted.

Mrs. Lee shook her head with a chuckle, and I realized that was obviously not what she was talking about.

"Oh . . . you mean America," I realized.

Mrs. Lee nodded. "I still remember the exact date I met Roger. My husband. March 17, 1971. I was twenty-three years old and working part-time at a restaurant near an American military base on the south coast. Of Korea, that is. He came in, ordered the *jjajangmyeon*, and told me I had the prettiest smile he had ever seen. I told him that I was just about to say the same thing about him." Mrs. Lee grinned. "From there, it felt like I was living in a romance book. Every weekend, we would explore a different coffee shop together, and during his time off, we even traveled to Jeju Island for a week. Of course, my parents were a little wary of a military man . . . but they liked that he was Korean American, and my siblings liked that he brought them gifts whenever he visited. It was a happy time."

Mrs. Lee sighed wistfully, fogging up her glasses. "But then his deployment ended. . . . "

"Oh," I said. "And *that's* when you moved here?"

Mrs. Lee nodded. "It wasn't an easy decision to make. I knew he was the one for me, but at the same time, I didn't want to leave my family behind. Or my home. I loved both of them so much."

Mrs. Lee looked down to hide the pain in her face, and my stomach shifted with guilt. I hadn't ever thought about her family before. I mean, I knew she must have had one—everyone did—but I hadn't wondered where they lived or what had happened to them. In fact, I had never really thought about Mrs. Lee's life at all.

I leaned back to examine her face—her wrinkled cheeks, her painted-on eyebrows, the white roots in her dyed black hair—trying to picture what she might have looked like when she was twenty-three. A carefree waitress with a mischievous glint in her eyes and a pretty smile.

"Do you ever regret the choice you made?" I asked after a long moment.

Mrs. Lee cocked her head to the side, deliberating my question.

"There have been points in my life, yes," she finally said. "Times when I felt isolated and alone, or when people treated me like I didn't belong. And sometimes just because. The first Christmas I spent here, I remember sobbing. It wasn't that I was unhappy—it was just that I missed my family so *much*."

"Did you ever go back to visit?"

"In the beginning we couldn't afford it, and by the time we did have the money for the trip, my parents had died. And then Roger got sick and died, too."

"That's really sad," I said. Without thinking, I reached out to take Mrs. Lee's hand.

She squeezed mine gently. "That's why I feel so blessed to have you three," she told me.

For a moment, we stared at each other in silence—Mrs. Lee lost in her memories, and me thinking hard about everything she had just told me . . . and the truly horrible thought that I had wanted to banish her upstairs for our party.

Then Mrs. Lee snorted. "Oh, look at me! Blabbering your ear off, and you were the one who came to me for advice. Now, what were you going to ask me, dear?"

"Oh!" I exclaimed, startled. For a moment, I had completely forgotten why I came to Mrs. Lee in the first place. Now it all rushed back to me. Helen. The dress. The enormous amount of money I owed her. The party. "That! I was going to ask you about . . . " But then I trailed off.

Because how was I supposed to tell Mrs. Lee all the ways she had ruined my life right after she had finished pouring her heart out to me?

"Uh, I was just going to ask you about . . . your. . . um . . . er . . . fantastic taste in lipstick!" I declared. "You always pick the perfect shades. Cherry red, wine mauve. So classy! And I wanted to know what brand you use. So that I can get some. For me. Um, when I'm allowed to wear makeup, that is."

Even as I said it, I knew it made almost no sense. Mrs. Lee tilted her head to one side and studied me, and I thought she was going to tell me I was talking gibberish. But then she smiled. It was a soft, kind smile, not like her usual molar-baring grin.

"Of course, dear. Now, pay attention, because here's the best advice I can give you: Sometimes you have to try a lot of things—even things that don't suit you at all—before you can know what really works for you."

"Okay," I said, slightly baffled.

"Good. Let's find you a color." Picking up her purse from the coffee table, she rummaged through it, muttering things like "This brand is cheaper but has less staying power" and "But this one might match your undertones more" and "Of course, this one is a Korean brand, and you know we have to support our own."

Finally, she pulled out a half dozen tubes of lipstick and shoved them into my hands.

"Try them all on!" she encouraged me. "Let's see which one is truly you."

I headed to the bathroom and pulled the door closed behind me. Uncapping each of the lipsticks in turn, I fanned them out and held them up to my face. I wasn't even sure why I was doing it, except that I didn't want to disappoint Mrs. Lee.

I stared at myself in the mirror, noticing the dark bags underneath my eyes and the paleness of my cheeks. That deep red shade would make me look like a vampire, I thought. Maybe that's truly me—a wicked bloodsucker.

"You know," Mrs. Lee called through the door, "my mother never let me wear lipstick at all. But I sneaked a tube in my pocket every time I knew I was going to see Roger."

The picture of young Mrs. Lee swam up in my mind's eye again, this time wearing cherry-red lipstick, smiling up at her Korean American boyfriend—who, I noticed with a slight shock, looked a lot like Marvel Moon. At least, in my imagination he did.

My heart lifted a little. Was it the thought of Marvel? Or did Mrs. Lee have some kind of weird cheer-up effect on me?

Setting down the rest of the tubes, I brought "Cherry-Oh Baby" to my lips and began stroking it on. I didn't do a very good job—I didn't really know how to put makeup on well—but as the bright color bloomed on my mouth, my spirits rose another notch. I capped the tube and opened the door. "So what do you think?" I asked Mrs. Lee, smiling.

She clasped her hands. "It's you, Pippa! Absolutely you!"

15

BIANCA

13 Days Until Christmas Eve

(I'm Feeling Superstitious . . .)

"So it turns out my mom and dad have an ulterior motive for this ski trip," Starsie announced.

The six of us were at our usual lunch table, and although normally this was one of my favorite parts of the school day, today I kept glancing at the clock, hoping the lunch bell would ring before anyone asked me for details about the party.

"What do you mean?" Win wanted to know.

"Apparently the resort we're going to is where they met, and they're planning to renew their wedding vows!" Starsie said. Her eyes sparkled. "It's kind of goofy, but also super adorable, don't you think?"

We all oohed and aahed, except Bianca, who was scrolling through her phone and didn't look up.

Starsie noticed Bianca's lack of attention, too. "Are you even listening, B?" she asked, pretending to pout.

Bianca glanced up. "That's great," she said with a tight smile. "Really sweet."

Starsie's smile faded and she looked a little hurt.

"Oh, a reminder for everyone," Helen said quickly. "Don't forget—it's Buddy's Hanukkah party next Wednesday. And you're all coming, right?"

My eyebrows raised. Or course I knew about Buddy's Hanukkah party—it was an annual tradition, and I hadn't missed one yet—but I didn't know he had invited all the Royals. Did he even want them there? It was hard to picture Buddy and Caroline sharing oxygen in the same room.

Caroline cleared her throat, like she was thinking the same thing. "Is this an optional excursion?" she asked. "Because it's Yoga Sunset Night at my gym, and I could really use it."

"Come on, Caroline," Starsie said.

"What? It does wonders for my posture. Seriously. I get like an inch taller."

"This is important to me," Helen said. "It's my first time meeting Buddy's family! And all his Victoria Middle friends will be there. And I won't know any of them. I *need* my friends by my side."

Caroline groaned. "Fine. I'll show—because I love you, or whatever. But if anyone posts a picture of me, I will sue for defamation." Caroline's gaze landed on me, slowly sizzling my corneas. "I do *not* 'hang out' with Victoria Middle misfits." She looked back over at Helen apologetically. "Except for your boyfriend, of course."

Helen ignored the dig. "Well, that's settled. So, let's move on. How's the party shaping up, Pips? Do you need help with the decorations?"

"Yeah, what's the theme?" Caroline chimed in.

I winced, feeling betrayed by Helen even though I knew her question was innocent. "Umm . . . things are moving along," I said, trying to keep my voice neutral. "I have some red and green streamers, and I was thinking of cutting up some paper snowflakes to hang on the windows."

"And?"

"And?" I repeated. From the look on Caroline's face, I realized that a pack of streamers from the Dollar Store wasn't going to cut it. "Well, uh, I was planning on going to the store this weekend," I lied. "To pick up everything else. So, I'll know more then."

Why did I just say that? I swallowed, and the stone inside me doubled in size. It wasn't just that I had no money. It was that I had *negative* money. I'd confessed to Helen that I

169

couldn't pay her back yet, and she had agreed to cover me until I could, but after that, I still needed to find a way to cover food costs. Not to mention the problem of the place . . . I stifled a groan. The stone was growing bigger by the second.

"If you want, I can bring over some of the decorations I used last year," Bianca offered.

For a moment, I just stared at her, eyes wide and jaw low. I knew I must have looked like a carp with my mouth hanging open like that, but I was still trying to process what Bianca had just said. Decorations? Bring? To me?

"That's . . . really nice of you," I finally spluttered.

And I truly meant it, but I couldn't help the tinge of suspicion in my voice. It had only been a month ago that Bianca seethed with resentment because of Eliot; now she wanted to help me? I stared into her intense gray eyes, trying to see if this was a trick, but if it was, she was doing a good job hiding it.

She shrugged. "They're just sitting around my house, taking up space."

I took a deep breath and wiped my sweaty palms on my pants. No more worrying about decorations! Of course, decorations didn't matter if you had nowhere to hang them. . . .

"Why don't I bring them over tonight?" she added.

"Ooo-kay," I said. A vision of Bianca coming into my apartment and seeing Mrs. Lee camped out in her bed made sweat break out along my hairline. I'd have to meet her in front of the building. "Just, um, text me when you're getting close. You know, like a few blocks away. So I'm sure I'll be there . . . because I never know where I'll be . . . but I won't be far . . . because where else would I be. . . ." *Stop rambling, Pippa.* I smiled at Bianca. "Uh . . . okay?"

"Sure," she said, giving me a faintly puzzled look.

"What about entertainment?" Caroline asked. "Last year we screened a bunch of holiday movies in Bianca's media room."

I gulped. "I haven't really gotten that far," I said.

Win gave me a little smile of support. Her family wasn't wealthy. Media rooms weren't part of her world either. "So—who's your date for the party?" she asked me, trying to change the subject.

Bianca glanced up from her phone, her gaze suddenly, sharply focused on me. Uh-oh. I was in enough potential hot water with the Royals—I didn't want to give Bianca any doubt about me and Eliot. Not that there was any, unfortunately.

"Um, I'm thinking about asking this guy, Marvel."

"Marvel? That's a funny name!" Starsie laughed.

"Starsie," Win chided her.

"What?" Starsie asked, her eyes widening. "It is. He sounds like a comic book character. Does he have super-powers?"

"Is he your boyfriend?" Bianca asked, ignoring Starsie.

"No. No. We're just friends." Bianca's laser-like gaze was still locked on me. "For now. But who knows?"

"Oh my god, look at your face." Caroline tittered. "If he's just a friend, why do you look like you're about to combust?"

"Do you *wish* he was your boyfriend?" Starsie waggled her eyebrows. Each of the Royals stared at me expectantly.

"Well . . . maybe," I said. "I mean, I like him, and he likes me. Or, at least, I think he does. He gives me a lot of attention when we're together and laughs at my jokes . . . but maybe he's just a friendly person to everyone?"

The group nodded thoughtfully, taking in this new information.

Bianca was the first to break the silence. "There's only one way to find out," she declared.

"I know, I know," I sighed. "I have to ask him if he likes me."

"Excuse me? *Absolutely* not!" Her nostrils flared.

I stared blankly at her and she sighed. "Pippa. What if it turns out he doesn't like you back? Then you would completely lose the high ground."

"The high ground?"

"It means you keep your pride," Caroline told me.

It sounded a little ridiculous to me, but the rest of the table seemed to understand what Bianca and Caroline were talking about.

"B and C are right," Starsie chimed in sagely. "It's sad when you like someone, and they don't like you back. But it's a million times worse when someone doesn't like you back but also knows that *you* like *them*." A small shudder rocked through her. "It's my worst nightmare."

"But if you're not supposed to ask, then what do you do?" I asked, bewildered.

"You're *supposed* to flirt," Caroline said.

"What does that even *mean*?" I asked.

"It means you put on something nice and make sure to borrow some mascara." Caroline sighed.

"Don't listen to her," Bianca said, earning a huff from Caroline. Now that she knew I was crushing on someone other than Eliot, she seemed more than happy to offer advice. "Boys don't like it when you give them all your attention. Of course, you still have to make a move. Otherwise, you could lose him completely. But be subtle."

"Or you can just tell him that you like his hair," Starsie added. We all raised our eyebrows at her. "What?" she asked. "Boys like compliments, too. I have a ninety percent success rate with that line."

I looked at Win, waiting for her to chime in, but she just shrugged. "I don't know if I'm the best person to give advice," she said. "Maybe try a lot of eye contact?"

Surprisingly, all the other girls nodded again, like this was obvious.

I was pretty certain that once I told Marvel that Buddy wasn't my boyfriend, he'd agree to come to the party, but a few dating tips couldn't hurt. Maybe I'd try some of them out Sunday night at rehearsal.

"Thanks," I said. "I'll let you know how it goes."

. . .

I had just started heating up a pot of creamy *chapag-etti* for me and Mrs. Lee when Bianca texted me a single word: **Downstairs.**

Nooo! She was supposed to text me when she was close.

Abandoning the pot on the stove, I tugged on my jacket and hurried down the steps. Bianca was sitting in the passenger seat of her dad's sleek black Range Rover when I walked outside, but once she spotted me, she climbed out, carrying an enormous cardboard box.

"Hey," I said. "Thanks for dropping this off." I reached for the box, but she held onto it.

"It's not heavy. I can handle it," she told me. "Will you just get the door?"

"Uh, the door?"

"Yeah, the door," Bianca repeated. She looked like she was resisting the urge to roll her eyes. "I can walk through it and carry this up to your apartment."

174

"Riii-iiight," I said. But I didn't move an inch.

Bianca tried to take a step past me, and I squeaked out, "No! Um, I mean, no . . . that's not necessary. We had a really hard practice today, and I'm sure you're exhausted, and really I can just bring up the box myself—no *problemo!*"

"I'm not tired at all," Bianca countered. She tried to move past me again, but I quickly shifted to the left. "Besides, it can't hurt for me to take a look around your apartment. We can decide where we want to hang up the tinsel, and if any of the colors don't work, I'll get more."

"That sounds amazing! Except—"

Except what? What could possibly be the exception to that?

"The thing is . . . " I opened my mouth. I had no idea what was about to come out, but I absolutely couldn't let Bianca into my apartment while Mrs. Lee commandeered the living room. "Well, you see, my sister has a friend who's staying at my apartment for a day or two. And she'll totally be gone by the party, so no worries there, but the thing is, she has a cat, and, well, you know, allergies are just a really big concern right now."

"But I'm not allergic to cats," Bianca said. "My uncle has two."

"Oh, I didn't mean that you'd be allergic to the cat!" I said hastily. "I meant the cat might be allergic to you! Or, er, not *you* specifically! Just, in general, he doesn't react well

175

to people—I mean, new people. He starts barfing everywhere and his eyes go kind of crossed, and, uh, we're trying really hard to find medication for him, but the vet didn't have any appointments open—and, anyways, it's just a huge, complicated . . . thing," I finished.

It was by far the most absurd thing I had ever said, but once I started speaking, there was no stopping me, and afterward I had no choice but to own it. I stared at Bianca, and Bianca stared back at me, and inside, I tried to keep myself from dying.

"I see," Bianca said after a long silence. "In that case, I guess you really should take up the box. Because of your cat. Who is allergic. To me."

"Right," I nodded emphatically.

"And you're sure everything's okay?"

"What? Of course!" I laughed. "A hundred and twenty thousand percent."

Bianca stared at me with those impenetrable eyes for another minute, and then she shrugged. "In that case, I guess I'll be going." She looked at the dark-tinted windows of her dad's car and then turned back to me. "Pippa . . . thank you."

"Of course, I—wait, what was that?"

"I said, 'Thank you,'" Bianca repeated. "I know Caroline is being a little bit of a pain about everything, so I just wanted to say thank you for handling this."

I waited for the nasty follow-up or the "but," only it didn't happen. Apparently, Bianca was being sincere. And it would have made me feel over the moon—if I wasn't on the verge of messing things up so badly with her and everyone else.

"Anyway, I'll see you Monday. Let me know if you need any help." She cleared her throat and her shoulders bunched up a little, like she wanted to say something more. "Bye, Pippa."

She turned back to her car, and for a fleeting second, I thought about calling out to her. Maybe this was the time to tell her the truth about the party—that I really, truly did need help.

Of course, I didn't say anything.

I watched her slowly open the door, climb in, and disappear. Then I slumped back against the brick wall of my apartment building, my breath rushing out in a plume of disappointment.

I'd had the chance to ask Bianca for help, but I hadn't taken it. I *couldn't* take it. And I had no idea why.

I shook my head. I was always trying to prove myself to the Royals—always insisting that I could handle everything. And look where it had gotten me. My insecurities had pushed me to this cliff, and now that I was here, I didn't know how to get back down. Ignoring the pounding in my temples,

I carried the box upstairs and into my room. I cracked open the top—and stared at enough tinsel to decorate a football stadium. The box had everything. Gold streamers, sparkling fairy lights, artificial green garlands . . . there were even the gold-plated snowflakes Caroline had sent me photos of from the department store.

Bianca had brought me a treasure trove!

Unfortunately for all of us, I had nowhere to put them.

16

ASSESS AND ADAPT

Only 10 Days Until Christmas Eve
(And Trying Hard Not to Think About It)

As I walked into the church on Sunday evening, my phone chirped at me. I pulled it out and frowned at the notification. I had a voice mail? No one left me voice mails. Not even Mina, since she always complained that I never checked them.

What was my password again? As I tried punching in numbers, I could hear angry voices on the stage.

"It's all her fault!"

"We don't want her on our team anymore."

Yikes, that sounded bad. Maybe I shouldn't go inside just yet. . . . Stopping outside the sanctuary, I perched on a chair and tried another number combination. Yes! It worked.

I pressed the phone to my ear . . . and my heart practically exploded as I heard the most wonderful voice mail ever.

"Miss Park? This is Joanne at the Blue Room." That was one of the party spaces I'd called. "I wanted to let you know that we just had a cancellation on December 24, so if you're still interested in our space, it is available."

"Yes!" I yelled, pumping my fist. "Yes, yes, yes!"

"Please call me back to discuss details. I'm leaving in just a few minutes, but you should be able to reach me tomorrow, any time after four p.m."

I strode into the rehearsal feeling as if I could jump over all the chairs in a single bound. I had a party space! Of course, it was probably going to be expensive, but I would figure that part out. In the worst-case scenario, I could ask the Royals to chip in—fifty bucks each would probably cover it—with a promise to pay them all back over time. I could earn enough from babysitting to pay everyone back in a couple of months.

I had a party space!

Onstage, voices were raised and every face I saw wore a scowl. As I walked closer to the disgruntled pageant group, Annie pointed a finger at Jewel. "Stop bragging about being Mary. The sheep are important, too."

"Girls!" Pastor Oh rushed over, his big brown eyes blinking rapidly. For a moment, the auditorium fell silent as everyone whipped around to look at him. "Pippa, they've been at it all afternoon, rehearsal is falling apart, and I have to tend to the scenery. If you can fix this . . . " he waved a hand, drawing an imaginary circle around the girls, " . . . it will be nothing short of a miracle." He walked to stage left, shouting, "More hay! Much more hay!"

I let out a sigh. I really, really wanted to find Marvel, but this would have to come first. And anyway, the way I was feeling right now, these kids would be putty in my hands.

"Well, it *is* her fault!" Annie exclaimed, at the same time Jewel shouted, "She started it!"

"Pippa, you said we're all on the same team," Annie huffed. "But she doesn't act like it."

"All right." Putting on my best Coach Ahmad voice, I said, "Being on a team means you talk to each other. Now, one at a time, let's start. Annie, you go first."

It turned out that jealousy was the cause of it all— Jewel was jealous of Annie because she got to be in charge of the sheep, and Annie was jealous of Jewel because she was playing Mary. I finally got them to agree that everyone's role mattered, and peace was restored.

Pastor Oh gave me a relieved and jovial grin. "That was amazing!" he told me.

"Nothing to it," I replied, and hurried backstage to where I thought I'd find Marvel.

There he was, sitting on the floor, leaning against a wall. He was wearing a black sweatshirt and had large white headphones wrapped around his neck, and even though his hair was all mussed up like he had just taken a nap, he somehow looked even cuter than the last time I had seen him. My chest started to ache the more I stared at him, and I realized it was because I had forgotten to breathe.

Which was practically the same feeling I had when I was with Eliot, I realized.

How can you really like two guys this much at the same time—two guys who are so totally different? I didn't understand it, but maybe the Royals would. *They have much more experience with these things than I do,* I thought, and that's when I remembered their flirting tips.

Okay, here goes. Don't start with the Buddy-not-your-boyfriend thing, I told myself. *That might make you look too interested. Play it cool.*

"Hey," I said. "Weird rehearsal, right?"

"Pretty much a train wreck till you showed up," Marvel agreed, and I tried to ignore the fuzzy feelings that passed through me.

"You think so?"

I knew it was pathetic, but I wanted to hear him say it again.

"Are you kidding me? Of course!" Marvel said. "I tried to step in and almost got my nose bitten off. Annie might only come up to my hip, but she's freaking terrifying."

I laughed.

But now it was time to let him know Buddy wasn't my boyfriend, and I suddenly felt nail-bitingly nervous. I took out my phone, pretending I had just received a text. "Oh, it's just from my friend Buddy. My good friend. No feelings between us. Well, just good-friend feelings. In fact, he's dating my best friend! I kinda helped introduce them."

This was not sounding cool.

"Oh," Marvel said.

"Yeah. So, no boyfriend currently. Or, I mean, in the foreseeable future, either." I paused. I didn't want him to interpret that as me not wanting a boyfriend. "Not that I would object to one!" I quickly added. "I'm not a nun or anything. Although nuns are great, I bet—no offense to them, I love *The Sound of Music*. It's just not the life for me. For a lot of reasons, but also because, yes, I do want a boyfriend. Eventually. Not right this second. I mean, I'm ready for it, but what I'm trying to say is it's not like I'm asking you to be my boyfriend or something. Ha ha, that would be ridiculous. Right?"

I bit my lip so that I would stop speaking and snuck a glance at Marvel from the corner of my eye. He had a small smile on his face, which I hoped meant that he was happy that I wasn't dating anyone—but then again, it could also just mean he was laughing at me.

"Good to know," Marvel finally said.

My heart thumped in my chest. *Good to know?* What was *that* supposed to mean? Did it mean he'd say yes this time if I asked him to the party?

Slow down, Pippa. I could practically hear Bianca's voice in my head. *You don't want to seem too eager.*

On stage, I heard Jewel say, "We've traveled so far, Joseph. How much farther until we find somewhere that will open its doors to us?"

My heartbeat sped up, drowning out the rest of her lines. In just a few minutes, Mary and Joseph would find a manger to stay in, and that would be the cue for Marvel and me to head onstage. There would be no time for talking for the rest of rehearsal, and afterward, Peter would find Marvel, and the two of them would head out to their mom's car, and Marvel would be gone, and I would spend the next week thumping my head against my bedroom wall, wondering what "good to know" meant.

Maybe flirting would seal the deal. I remembered Bianca's advice—tease him a little.

"You know, you're a little bit of a goofball," I blurted out. "I was, uh, just thinking that."

"I'm a . . . goofball?" Marvel repeated.

I could tell by his tone that my first attempt at flirting wasn't winning any awards. Maybe Starsie's approach?

"But you have really good hair. Even when you have bedhead."

184

"Um, thanks? I guess?" He squinted as if he was trying to see me clearer. "Are you okay, Pippa? You're acting a little . . . strange."

Strange?

This wasn't working.

Just ask him to the party.

"Marvel, I—"

"I think that's our cue," he interrupted. "So you should probably head back to your side of the stage."

"Right." I sighed. "Guess I'll see you around."

"I'd like that," Marvel said. "Maybe at Duo's?"

For a moment, I just stared at him. Because what else was I supposed to do? Had Marvel seriously asked me out on a date? Or was he just making fun of me?

"What? Together?" I sputtered.

"Yeah," Marvel said, grinning. "It'd be fun to see you someplace that's not here. You in? Maybe Tuesday after school? I've got to watch Peter until my mom gets home from work. So how is six fifteen?"

"Um—sure!" I couldn't believe it. This would be my first actual date. And in between laughing and endless amounts of ice cream, I'd ask him to come to the party. And I knew this time he'd say yes.

Things were starting to come together!

Perfect party space: check (almost).

Perfect party dress: check.

Perfect decorations: check.

Perfect date: check (almost).

Everything finally falling into place: check.

. . .

Swish! The ball went through the net and Bianca pumped her fist, satisfied.

"Nice one," I congratulated her, and she grinned.

"Thanks. Hey, how's the allergic cat?" she asked me.

I blinked. This was the second time in less than a week Bianca had seemed downright friendly. "He's a giant pain," I admitted, thinking about Boz, and Bianca laughed out loud.

"What's so funny?" Caroline asked. Bianca and I were on the same team today, and Caroline was covering me.

"Oh, nothing," Bianca said carelessly. "You had to be there."

Caroline's eyes narrowed. But before she could say anything, Coach Ahmad blew a blast on her whistle. "Ten minutes on the clock, girls. Stay sharp!" she barked. "Remember—you're not on break yet, and I don't want to see anyone slacking!"

Even though the ball hadn't passed half-court, I bent my knees lower, and raised my arms higher. I would *not* be caught slacking. From my position on the three-point line,

I watched as Serena passed the ball to Helen, who passed it to Starsie, who passed it back to Serena, who passed it to Caroline. Caroline dribbled forward—zigzagging past Win and Kate—and headed straight for the hoop.

I sprinted forward. We were supposed to be practicing zone defense, but it was clear that Caroline was going to score if I didn't do anything.

"Nice decision, Park!" Coach called. "Assess and adapt, girls. Assess and adapt!"

Caroline made a face but was forced to dribble back a step. I stayed on her, not giving her any wiggle room. Her eyes darted back and forth between me and the hoop, searching for a way out. But there wasn't one.

"Over here!" Starsie shouted. "I'm open!"

Caroline's feline gaze shifted to the side. She liked to play aggressively and hated passing—but there was nothing else for her to do in this situation. My hips twitched to the left, ready to block her throw.

Only Caroline surprised me.

Instead of picking up the ball and passing, she made a break for it. Straight forward—into me.

Her shoulder rammed into mine, and I went sprawling across the court. Before I had the chance to register the pain, Coach blew her whistle.

"Bingham! That's a personal foul!"

"Sorry, Coach," Caroline called back. "Accident!" She gazed down at me, not sorry at all, and held out a hand. From my vantage point on the floor, she looked monstrously tall. "You understand, right, Pippa?"

"I understand. Totally."

I understand that you are the worst kind of person.

But I couldn't say that out loud—not when Caroline was batting her big eyes at me, pretending to be all innocent. And definitely not while everyone—including Coach—watched. Ignoring Caroline's hand, I climbed to my feet and massaged my sore shoulder.

"You good, Park?" Coach yelled.

Glaring at Caroline, I called, "Never been better."

After practice, I made a beeline for the locker room. I had a babysitting gig to get to, and I didn't want to be late. With today's money, I'd have enough to pay Helen back for the dress. Bianca headed for the bathroom, Helen to the shower, and I went straight to my locker. As I started to shimmy into my Lakeview skirt, Win sat on the bench next to me.

"You okay?" she asked. "Caroline rammed into you pretty hard."

Two lockers away, Caroline rolled her eyes. "Please, I barely tapped her," she said. "In fact, I was more surprised than anyone at how fast you dropped, Pippa." Caroline laughed, and my stomach clenched. I wanted to wipe that smile from her face. Instead, I turned back to my locker and pretended to rummage around for a textbook. If I didn't engage with Caroline, she would eventually stop talking. But even if I was done with the conversation, Win wasn't.

"Probably because she didn't expect her *friend* to attack her," Win argued. "You were playing dirty."

"I was playing *smart*." Caroline's nostrils flared and her hands balled up into fists. "In fact—"

But before Caroline could say anything else, Starsie draped an arm around my shoulder and frowned at her. "Oh, don't get salty, C," she said. Normally, her voice was light and airy, but today it bordered on chiding. "You were the one who went all feral on Pippa."

"Yeah, you're lucky Pippa's so chill," Win added. "If you tried that on one of us, you know we'd push back."

Caroline's mouth closed with a furious popping noise. She glared at me with a gaze as boiling hot as lava, but eventually shrugged. Apparently, she knew when she was outnumbered.

"All right," she said. "All of you are so sensitive. I was just joking. *Obviously.*"

When none of us said anything, she shook out her long mane of hair.

"Fine." She turned to me, her lips jutting forward petulantly. "I guess I'm sorry if I accidently hurt you. Okay?

Anyway," Caroline said, before I could respond, "let's talk about something actually important. When did you mail the invites, Pippa?"

"The invites?" I blinked at her, confused by the rapid change in subject.

"Uh, duh. For the party?" Caroline looked sharply at me. "I checked with my friend Veronica this morning, and she still hasn't gotten hers."

"Oh! *Those* invites. Of course." I laughed confidently, attempting to cover up my mistake, but my stomach clenched. The invitations had completely slipped my mind. And even if I had remembered them, it wasn't like I could have mailed them anyway. Not when I wasn't sure what address to put down for the party. But I couldn't tell the Royals that.

In fact, the cards and envelopes were still stuffed in the lower compartment of my backpack. I gripped the straps tighter, just in case Caroline used her Jedi mind powers to read my thoughts and tried to snatch them from me. Probably they were all wrinkled by now, and if she saw the state of them, I knew she would do more than shoulder-tackle me.

Trying not to panic as Caroline grew more impatient, I finally blurted, "Um, well, the reason Veronica hasn't gotten hers is because . . . no one has."

"Excuse me?"

"I saw these cute holiday stamps online, so I just had to put in an order!" I claimed. "It took forever to ship, but they, uh, finally got here last night, and so I was planning on stamping everything and mailing them tonight."

"Riii-iiight. The reason you haven't sent out the invites is because of . . . holiday stamps," Caroline repeated dubiously.

"Yeah! You know. They're stamps . . . but holiday themed! They have little snowflakes and reindeer on them. Stuff like that."

Caroline stared at me for so long that I could feel sweat bead up on the back of my neck. It seemed like hours passed before she rolled her eyes. "Pippa, there are exactly ten days left before the party. What if people made other plans? What if no one can make it now?" Her voice turned shrill.

"Calm down, Caroline." Helen came out from the shower, towel-drying her hair. "Everyone knows about the party. Everyone knows where and when it is."

"That's right," Win said. "We all told our guests about it. And I saw you send your guests save-the-date emails."

"That's not the point," Caroline huffed. "The Royals have standards. It's not the way we do things. We don't send out our invitations late." She turned abruptly and headed for the bathroom, ending my interrogation.

They told everyone the party is at my house. That was awkward. But assuming I would reach Joanne at the Blue Room after four today to confirm, I could fix it. It was a slipup but not a catastrophe.

191

Still, I was starting to get that knot in my stomach again. Caroline was right. Ten days *was* cutting it close. And what if the Blue Room was too expensive?

"Sorry that Caroline is being such a grump today," Starsie told me. "She's probably stressed about her family coming over. She has like seventeen cousins, and she hates all of them."

"Not that that's an excuse," Win emphasized. "But don't worry—the rest of us know you've got this!"

"Yeah!" Starsie squeezed my hand. "We believe in you!"

"Thanks," I said. "That means a lot."

And it did.

I just hoped I deserved their confidence.

And just like that, I was horribly nervous again. Disappointing them would be terrible. And Caroline would be joyous. I could hear her now: "I told you she couldn't do it. I told you she wasn't Royal material." Suddenly, my fingers felt like ice.

Swallowing my worry, I waved goodbye to Win and Starsie and headed to the exit. As I walked out, I spotted Helen and Bianca in the corner of the locker room. Their heads were bent low toward each other, and they were speaking so softly that I couldn't hear what they were saying. I watched Helen glance over at me—but before I could wave, she looked away, and whispered something in Bianca's ear.

I froze. Were they talking about *me*?

Helen wouldn't, part of me argued. *She's not like that.*

But when Bianca also glanced back at me, my stomach took a dive.

What if Bianca had told Helen how weird it was that I wouldn't let her upstairs to my apartment the other day? Maybe she asked Helen if she'd noticed anything strange about me lately. From there, it would be natural for Helen to tell Bianca about how I owed her money, and how I hadn't been able to pay her back yet.

And now they were probably wondering if I was lying about the invitations.

Tucking my head down, I hurried out of the locker room.

At the bike rack, I fumbled with my bike, my pulse pounding in my ears. Why, why, why had I ever thought I could really fit in with the Royals? How could I ever live up to their standards? It was obvious that Caroline didn't think I could.

But Helen? Helen, who called me Pips and laughed at the same things I did? It really hurt to think she was talking about me behind my back.

Calm down, Pippa, I told myself. *You don't know what they were saying. They could have been talking about anything.*

But as I pedaled to my babysitting gig, I felt lonelier than ever.

17

DOUBLE TROUBLE

Only 9 Days Left Until Christmas Eve
(How? Just How?)

By the next day, I was feeling a little better. I hadn't been able to speak to Joanne at the Blue Room, but I left a message with all the details with her assistant, who seemed to think there would be no problem. Joanne just had to get back to me with a final price. The assistant promised she would text it to me sometime today.

Plus, today was my date with Marvel. It was going to take place in T-minus two hours and forty-three minutes, and I was sure the whole school could hear my heartbeat hammering away beneath my Lakeview blazer. My first date! Ever! I wanted to shout it to the moon and back.

School was over for the day, but I didn't have to get to Duo's until six fifteen. More than enough time to go home and change out of my school uniform. As I piled my notebooks into my backpack, I felt a tap on my shoulder.

"Hey, Pippa."

It was Eliot.

For a moment, the sight of him short-circuited my brain, and all I could do was stare. His Lakeview uniform was perfectly pressed today, and his hair looked so impossibly fluffy that I had to clench my hands into fists just to resist the temptation to touch it.

T-minus two hours and thirty-nine minutes now, I reminded myself sternly. *Control yourself!*

"Hey," I said, casually. Trying to play it cool, I shoved the rest of my books into my backpack, then swung my locker shut so that I could lean back against it. "What's up?"

"Nothing much," he said. "Well, actually, there is something. Obviously, since I'm standing in front of your locker." He scratched the back of his head, looking a little embarrassed. "That came out kind of strange."

I raised my eyebrows. Usually, *I* was the bumbling one in our conversations. Was this what I sounded like?

"Anyway." Eliot straightened his shoulders. "I was just wondering if you wanted to hang out today."

The next five seconds took a small eternity to pass as I stared, open-mouthed, at him.

"*What?*" I finally croaked.

"There's this holiday music recital thing going on at the mall, and my brother Matthew is actually playing in it. You remember Matthew, right?"

"I—of course I do! Who wouldn't remember the

guy in the woods with the violin?" I babbled. "I mean, that sounds kind of creepy, but Matthew's not creepy. At all. I like Matthew."

I winced, expecting Eliot to give me one of his stony stares, the way he had last time I tried to joke with him. But he didn't. He gave a little chuckle.

"Yeah, well, he likes you, too. In fact, he asked about you. So I figured I'd invite you. Also, I, uh, wanted to say sorry," Eliot added. "For my great-aunt. I should have apologized sooner, but I was kind of embarrassed."

"Oh. But that wasn't your fault!" I told him. "I mean, your Aunt Evelyn makes my list of top-ten fears, and I'm not even related to her. She's terrifying! No offense."

Eliot gave me one of his rare, genuine smiles, and it melted me like butter in a warm pan. Which . . . was a problem. The bubble of helium that had been growing inside me popped suddenly.

Because no matter which way I looked at it, there was only one person whose smile I should be thinking about right now, and that was Marvel.

"Anyway, are you in? Snacks are on me."

Oh, man. Why couldn't this conversation have happened a week earlier?

"Well . . . the thing is . . . ," I started, then paused.

Because what was I *doing*? I mean, the most popular, smartest, *dreamiest* boy at Lakeview was asking if I—the girl who nearly fainted every time we had a conversation—wanted to hang out with *him*. It was a total no-brainer.

But Marvel . . .

What about him? I could practically feel the little devil sitting on my shoulder.

You'll hurt his feelings! wailed the angel on my other shoulder.

Pipe down, both of you! That was me—my own voice. *Just . . . just wait. Maybe this is okay. It's not like Eliot is asking me on a date. He said it himself—he wants to apologize. It's really more of an "I'm sorry" hangout than anything else. Besides, I'm not supposed to meet up with Marvel for at least two more hours. That's plenty of time!*

"The thing is?" Eliot repeated.

"The thing is . . . uh . . . that I have to work on some party stuff later tonight!" I lied. "So, I have to be home by six. If that's okay."

"Good with me. Let's do it."

As we walked over to the bus stop, I tried to smother the guilt fermenting the contents of my stomach. I probably should have told Eliot about my date with Marvel, but I just couldn't. What if I told him and he was like, "Wait, you thought I was asking you on a *date*? Are you out of your mind?"

On the way to the mall, we talked about basketball and classes and how I was going to sleep a full twenty-four hours straight as soon as school let out—and Eliot laughed a total of three times on the ten-minute ride. A new record! Not that anyone was counting.

When we reached the mall, we headed to the second floor, over to the food court. Normally, the space was cramped and on the dirty side, but they had cleaned it up and moved around a bunch of chairs and tables for the occasion, and there was a tiny stage set up next to a glitzy, tinsel-covered Christmas tree. It felt less like a trip to the mall, and more like I was Eliot's special guest at a concert.

"I'll go grab some snacks," he said once we had staked out a table.

As I waited for him to return, I couldn't help but scan the crowd, searching for familiar faces from Lakeview. I didn't necessarily want to run into someone like, say, Bianca, who would definitely not be happy to see me with Eliot. But if I was going to be in public with Eliot, it wouldn't hurt to run into and impress at least a couple of eighth graders.

Unfortunately, I didn't recognize any of the faces surrounding me. Not that it stopped the tiny glow of pride I felt. Here I was, in public with Eliot, and I hadn't even had to trick him into it! And if Marvel's disapproving face happened to flash before me, the sight of Eliot wading through the crowd with a huge soft pretzel for us and a big grin was enough for me to push Marvel to the back of my mind.

As I stuffed warm, pillow-soft bites of salted pretzel into my mouth, the orchestra started up its first song, "It's

Beginning to Look a Lot Like Christmas." The mall was packed, but as soon as the violins started up—with Matthew right out in front—everyone went silent, even the toddlers.

The music was nice, but the real thrill came from sitting next to Eliot, with not a single textbook in sight. Unable to resist, I sneaked a quick glance at him. His blue eyes were focused on his brother, and he bobbed his head lightly to the beat. He looked . . . relaxed, I decided.

A grin spread across my face just as the orchestra transitioned to "All I Want for Christmas Is You," and Eliot glanced my way. Embarrassed to be caught staring, I hastily looked away. But in my peripheral vision, I could see Eliot smiling, too, and it made my heart flutter in ways that couldn't be healthy.

Stop it, I told myself. *Stop it this instant. Marvel is the one who's supposed to make your heart flutter! And he does!*

Despite that, when the concert ended, I couldn't help the twinge of disappointment that coursed through me—I was having such a good time.

Matthew loped over to our table. "Hey, Pippa Park!" he greeted me. "Thanks for coming!"

"You sound as good as ever," I told him.

He grinned. "I'm working on it. Listen, sorry I can't stick around—we have to run right over to a gig at a nursing home. But I hope I see you over the break. Catch you at home, Eliot," he said and hurried away.

As people began gathering their things, I looked over at Eliot and saw that he was gazing at the carousel at the other end of the food court.

"I used to love riding that! My favorite was the black horse. Although it's been forever since I've been on it," I told him impulsively. "Jung-Hwa used to bring me here, and I'd pretend I was a bandit from one of those western movies, fleeing from the law. I would even wear a cowboy hat, which I begged Mina to buy specifically for this ride. And actually, now that I'm saying it out loud, it's really embarrassing, and I have no idea why I'm telling you any of this," I added, going crimson.

But instead of making fun of me, Eliot grinned. He grabbed my hand and jumped to his feet.

"What are you doing?" I asked, trying to ignore how soft his hand was and the way it was actually and really touching mine.

"I never rode the carousel before," he told me. "My dad never let me. He said it was a waste of a dollar. But after hearing that, now I *have to.*"

Without waiting for an answer, Eliot tugged me toward the ride. He seemed really excited as he bought two tickets from the machine. I scrambled onto my old friend, a glossy black steed with blue marble eyes, and Eliot hopped onto a gray rhino next to me. We were the oldest kids there, but as soon as the campy carnival music started and our animals glided up along their posts, both of us were laughing and whooping like we were little again.

Even after we stumbled off, Eliot wore a huge smile. Without thinking, I told him, "You act different outside of school."

"Oh yeah?"

"Yeah. Happier," I said.

Instantly, I cringed, realizing how rude that sounded. But Eliot didn't look angry. Instead, he grinned even wider.

"I guess I am happy," he said, and my heart felt like it grew twice its size. "Speaking of which, I'm not ready to go home yet. Why don't we go to Duo's?"

And just like that, my heart began to shrivel.

Duo's! Marvel! *Marvel*. What time was it? I grabbed my phone and saw that it was nearly six. I was supposed to meet Marvel at Duo's in twenty minutes!

"I'm sorry," I said. "But—"

"I know, I know. You have party stuff to plan," Eliot said. "So maybe it's selfish of me to ask. But . . . I like spending time with you," he admitted, his eyes darting briefly toward his shoes. "It's fun."

I had no idea what to do. This was no longer just an apology hangout—Eliot *wanted* to keep spending time with me. And he wanted to take me to Duo's, the most popular diner in town. We were sure to run into somebody we knew there. How was I supposed to pass up the opportunity to drink hot cocoa with the most popular boy at Lakeview? There were at least 170 other girls who would literally kill to be in my place right now!

And if I said no, this opportunity might never come again.

I bit my lip, weighing my options. Surely, Marvel would understand if I postponed our date by just a day or two?

Before I could think too hard, I whipped out my phone.

"I'm in," I told Eliot. "Just give me a second."

To Marvel, I texted: **I'm so sorry, but a last-minute thing came up. Can we reschedule for Thursday? I promise my knock-knock jokes will be of the highest quality!**

The tiny "message read" symbol appeared, then the three little white dots that meant he was typing. After a few seconds, the dots disappeared. Reappeared. And then vanished again. I was just starting to sweat when his reply came through.

No problem! Thursday.

I really am sorry, I texted back.

His second reply came almost immediately. **Seriously, don't sweat it. Life happens. Besides, I'll still be just as handsome on a Thursday as I am on a Tuesday.**

I snorted at his reply, and my stomach gave a guilty flip. Marvel was a genuinely good guy. He hadn't acted annoyed at me for canceling on him. Instead, he was cracking jokes to make *me* feel better. So what was I doing, going to the same restaurant we were supposed to meet at, but with a different boy?

"Everything okay?" Eliot asked, breaking through my uneasy thoughts.

"Huh? What? Oh! Yes! Of course, everything's okay. Why wouldn't it be?" I said. "We're just headed to Duo's. Nothing illegal with that! And even if it was illegal, that's only if you get caught, right? Ha ha. But like I said, no, there's nothing wrong."

Eliot gave me a strange look, and I forced myself to take a deep breath.

"Everything is perfect," I said firmly. "Let's go."

Five minutes later, we were on the bus downtown, and I was already feeling marginally better despite blowing Marvel off. I knew it wasn't the right thing to do—but he would never find out. And if it couldn't hurt him, then it wasn't too terrible. Right?

"Hey, look!" Eliot said.

I glanced out the window just in time to see a flurry of movie-perfect snowflakes drifting down from the charcoal sky.

It was the first snowfall of the winter—that had to be lucky. Maybe it was a sign I had made the right decision after all. The bus slid to a stop at the corner of Duo's, and I clambered down the stairs, my arms raised up toward the sky.

Eliot laughed as I caught snowflakes on my tongue, and for about three pure, joyous moments, everything was perfect.

And that's when someone called out, "Pippa?"

Immediately, I froze, tongue out, head tilted back. An icy wave of terror washed through me. *That isn't . . . that can't be . . .*

"Marvel?"

My head snapped forward just as he emerged from Duo's. He carried a small take-out container, and his dark hair was brushed back neatly behind his ears—no headphones in sight. He looked better than ever—and all I could do was stare at him in horror.

"What are you doing here?" I demanded.

"Me? I was just leaving," he said. "I got to Duo's a little early—okay, a lot early—and so I was already here when your text came in." He cocked his head. "But I could ask you the same question! I thought something came up—not that I'm not happy to see you."

"Right. About that . . . ," I hedged.

As I scrambled for something to say, Marvel's gaze flitted from me to Eliot. His eyes opened wide in confusion—before narrowing in realization. And just like that, all the warmth faded from his gaze.

"Oh," he said, his voice going flat. "So that's why."

"Wait! It's not like that!" I sputtered.

"Yeah? Then tell me what it's like," Marvel countered. He nodded at Eliot. "This is your boyfriend, Buddy, right?"

"No," I said, at the same time Eliot demanded, "Wait, you have a boyfriend named Buddy?"

"No," I repeated. I shook my head at Marvel. "I already told you that Buddy is just a friend—and that I don't have a boyfriend!"

I meant for my voice to come out hard and firm, but instead it was squeaky and soft. My hands were trembling, my face was flushed, and my head was spinning so fast I could barely think straight.

And neither Eliot nor Marvel looked like they believed I didn't have a boyfriend.

"Look," I said, my voice trembling. "I can explain—"

"Everything. I'm sure," Marvel said, with no hint of his signature humor. "You're great at explaining things. So go ahead . . . explain."

I swallowed. Marvel seemed furious. Eliot looked disappointed. And neither of them appeared to have any sympathy for me.

So I did the only thing I could think of. I tucked my hair back behind my ear, took a deep breath, opened my mouth, and blurted, "I have to go."

And then, before either of them could say anything, I raced off down the street.

I was almost halfway home when my phone buzzed.

Dreading to see who had texted me, I pulled out my phone with trembling fingers. Was it Marvel telling me that I was the worst person ever? Or Eliot demanding to know what had just happened? Both would be equally awful.

But it was neither of them.

It was a message from the party place. I stopped breathing as I read the message.

Dear Ms. Park,

We're delighted that you want to rent our space. As promised, here is our estimate.

Our minimum package is $30 per guest. For 32 guests, that comes to $960, or, with tax and gratuity, $1,254.50. We accept all major credit cards; please let us know how you'd like to pay.

Warm wishes for a joyous holiday,

The Blue Room Staff

18

HELLO, HANUKKAH,
GOODBYE, CHRISTMAS

Only 8 Days Until Christmas Eve
(And Until I Fall Off the Face of the Planet)

The next morning, I woke up to the sound of my alarm. The sun slanted merrily through the gaps in my blinds, reminding me that it was time to get up and seize the day. I groaned and buried my head underneath my pillow.

I couldn't do it. I could not leave my safe, cozy bed. Because if I did, then that meant it was time to get dressed, but if I got dressed, then the next step was heading to the school bus, and naturally the school bus would take me to Lakeview, and once I was at Lakeview I would have to go inside . . . only, that was impossible, because if I did go inside, then I would see Eliot and the Royals, and I couldn't face any of them. The most reasonable option was to drop out of school. But Mina

207

would never allow that. Maybe I could run away and join the circus?

I groaned louder. There was no sense in putting it off. I rolled out of bed and got ready for school.

An hour later, I stood in the entranceway.

Bach's Orchestral Suite No. 3 filled the air—that was Lakeview's version of the five-minute warning bell.

The thought of running into either Eliot or the Royals made my stomach do backflips. I knew I would have to tell the Royals about the party, and I knew Eliot would think I was a horrible person—and if he asked me for an explanation about last night, I had no idea what to say.

As I shuffled through the front doors, I kept my head down and my pace brisk. I ducked down a side hall and looped behind the cafeteria, taking the long route to my locker. By the time I reached it, the hallways were abandoned. I grabbed my stuff, shoved my backpack inside, and slid into my first class with only five seconds to spare. No time to talk to anyone.

Yet.

. . .

When lunchtime came around, my stomach was tied in one huge knot.

Eliot sat at his usual table, twirling spaghetti around a plastic fork as his friends flicked paper footballs at one another. He glanced up and caught my gaze, but his expression was unreadable. To the right, I saw the Royals seated at their usual table. They were laughing at something on Helen's phone—until Starsie waved and they all looked my way.

Well, this is it. There's no more hiding. Rubbing my sweaty hands on the sides of my blazer, I straightened my shoulders, steeled myself . . . and deflated.

I can't do this.

Giving an awkward half wave, I bolted. If they questioned me later, I would tell them I had a last-minute project due. Instead, I ate *kimbap* alone in one of the library's study pods. It was a lonely lunch, and only a temporary solution. Buddy's Hanukkah party was tonight, and I couldn't bail on him; it was a tradition, and I had to be there. So tonight was the night. Tonight I'd tell the Royals everything.

. . .

That night, as I made the short trek over to Buddy's house, my heart thrummed unevenly. I could already envision the disgusted way Bianca's nostrils would flare and how Caroline would shake her head and tell everyone who would listen, *"See? I told you Pippa would let us down. Obviously."* And Helen? What would she do? Even in my own imagination, I couldn't guess her expression. Would she look at me with pity or simply disappointment? Either one would be devastating.

I knocked on the door, and it swung open almost immediately.

"Pippa! You're here!" Helen said.

Behind her, Buddy grinned at me. "I was wondering when you'd roll through," he said. "Figures that you'd get here just in time for the first batch of latkes! Absolutely classic! Did you smell them from your apartment?"

Forcing a tiny grin, I followed Buddy and Helen into the house. As we passed the dining room, I waved to his parents. "Hi, Mr. and Mrs. Johnson!" They waved back, all smiles. It seemed like the entire family had made it out for the celebration. Buddy's two brothers, plus four uncles, three aunts, and seven cousins, were all crammed around the tiny dining room table, sharing platters of crispy golden latkes and baskets of sweet jelly donuts. They had already lit today's candle on the menorah, which sat at the center of the table with four flickering flames, three representing each day of Hanukkah that had already passed. A bowl filled with Hanukkah gelt— pieces of chocolate wrapped in gold foil to look like coins— sparkled in the candlelight.

Buddy had invited a few of his other friends, but there was no mingling between groups. The Lakeview Royals had staked out the area around the living room couch, the Victoria Middle School kids had claimed the spot in front of the television in the family room, and both circles seemed more than happy to keep it that way.

As Buddy went to cheer on his friend Jack during a round of *Mario Party*, Helen steered me toward the Royals.

"It seems like forever since we've hung out," she told me, squeezing my hand. "I've missed you!"

"I've missed you, too," I said, even though what I wanted to say was, *And whose fault is that?*

But I didn't have time for that right now. My prime mission was to tell the Royals that I couldn't throw the holiday party, and the sooner I did that, the sooner I could slink out of Buddy's house in shame.

"Hey, Pippa!" Starsie waved as I walked over. She and Win were sitting cross-legged on the floor, eating jelly donuts and giggling as they played with a red plastic dreidel. Up on the couch, Bianca smiled at something Caroline said. Moose, Buddy's Italian greyhound, was already curled up in her lap.

They all seemed perfectly happy—and I knew I was about to ruin that. I winced. Maybe this actually wasn't the best time to bring up my news. I had already destroyed the Royals' party. Did I really want to mess up Buddy's, too?

I took a shaky breath, and Helen noticed immediately. "Something wrong?"

"No, no," I said automatically. But then I cringed. I couldn't keep doing this. Even if it wasn't the best time, I *had* to come clean. "Well, actually, there is *something* that's on my mind. In fact, I'm glad you're all here, because I—"

"Hey, Helen, are you busy? I want to introduce you to

Aunt Ruth, Aunt Margie, and Uncle Rob before they head out," Buddy interrupted, coming up behind Helen and squeezing her shoulder. "And some of my cousins who just got here . . . "

"Why does she have to meet every single person in his family all in one night?" Bianca wrinkled her nose. Then she turned to me. "Anyway, sorry, Pippa, were you going to say something?"

Suddenly, all eyes were staring at me, and I had no idea how to start.

I know it's been nearly a month and I had at least a dozen opportunities to say something sooner, but . . .

I didn't want to let you down, because I really wanted to impress you all, and I've been trying so hard to make it work. . . . Look, I reached out to three different venues, and I kept waiting, hoping, that one would be available. . . . "Well?" Caroline arched an eyebrow.

"Um, yes. Yes, I was going to say . . . that . . . that I need to use the bathroom!" I blurted. "I've been drinking water nonstop today, and it's supposed to be great for cleansing your liver, but it also turns you into a human water fountain. Anyway, I'll be right back."

Ignoring the perplexed looks on my friends' faces, I leaped up and practically sprinted to the bathroom. I told myself I was just waiting for Helen to return, but I knew that wasn't the reason. Really, I was just a coward. Plain and simple.

I stared at myself in the mirror. My face was red and flushed, and my hair had started to frizz around the temples because of excess sweat. I looked exactly how I felt—like I was falling apart.

I turned on the faucet and splashed cool water on my face, reminding myself that no matter what happened, the Royals couldn't kill me. They could scream at me, kick me from our lunch table, make my life on the basketball team pure torment, and ruin every other part of my school life—but they wouldn't actually, physically murder me.

It wasn't a great comfort, but it was a start.

You don't want to do this, but you have to, I told myself.

Feeling like I was preparing for a game-day match, I grabbed the spare hair tie off my wrist and gathered my tangled hair into a ponytail. Then I used one of Mrs. Johnson's lavender-scented hand towels to dry off the rest of my face. It was time.

Straightening my shoulders, I pushed open the bathroom door. I walked to the end of the hallway and peered into the dining room. I wanted to find Helen before I made the official announcement. But she wasn't in the dining room or the living room.

I frowned just as I heard a shuffling noise coming from Buddy's room. *Oh, good,* I thought. *If anyone knows where Helen is, it's Buddy.*

213

Backtracking down the hallway, I peeked through Buddy's cracked door—and froze.

I had found Helen. And Buddy.

They were standing inside Buddy's room, and they were very close together. As I watched, Buddy laughed nervously, and Helen glanced down at the floor. And I knew—I really knew—I shouldn't be spying on them right now, but my feet seemed stuck to the floor. I couldn't have moved if I tried.

I watched as Buddy stepped forward. I watched as Helen brought her face closer to his.

And I watched as their lips met.

A heavy sadness fell over me. I couldn't help it—I felt like I had just lost my two best friends. They had gone somewhere I couldn't go—not with them, at least.

As they kissed, my thoughts drifted to Eliot and Marvel. And how I had ruined my chance of any kind of relationship with either of them.

I thought about how the Royals were about to dump me.

I thought about how I had never felt so alone.

How had my life turned into such a mess?

All at once, I just couldn't take it anymore. Couldn't face talking to anyone, not even to say I was leaving.

Turning, I tiptoed down the hall and quietly fled out the back door of Buddy's house.

19

HUMBUG

Only 7 Days Until Christmas Eve

(Not That It Matters Now ...)

"Pippa! How could you do that?"

"What?" I said, turning to see Helen approaching our lockers. It was the day after Buddy's party. Science class had just ended, and I had bolted as soon as the bell rang, trying to avoid her.

"How could you forget to write your science paper? It counts for one-third of our grade. It's a good thing Mr. Donoghue said you could hand it in late." She seemed to be studying my face. "Is everything okay?" she asked.

"Why wouldn't it be?" I replied.

"I mean, you seemed a little out of it during class. And last night, you left Buddy's house as soon as you got there! I barely saw you."

"Oh," I said. "Right."

I took a deep breath. Now would be the right time for me to tell Helen the truth—about everything. Like how I kept procrastinating with the holiday party until I felt too overwhelmed to tell anyone. And how that had snowballed into a disaster. Or how I had ruined my chances with both Eliot and Marvel. Or maybe just how much I missed hanging out with her one-on-one, and how I was worried we were drifting apart.

That's what I wanted to say.

Only, when I looked at Helen, all I could see was a repeat of last night—Buddy and Helen leaning in, their smiles nervous and excited as they brought their faces closer. Immediately, my stomach felt tight and my neck hot. Logically, I knew Helen and Buddy's relationship shouldn't bother me. Helen was dating. It's exactly what I wanted to be doing. And it shouldn't matter that she was dating Buddy. But their kiss made me feel abandoned and like I was completely falling behind. Like, Helen was walking away from me, up a flight of stairs, and I was just tumbling down, down, down. . . .

And so instead of saying what I wanted, I just shook my head and zipped up my backpack.

"Wait," Helen said, her tone changing. "Are you . . . mad at me?"

"No!" I said, too forcefully. "No," I repeated. "It's just that . . . it feels like a lot of things are changing."

"What things?" Helen frowned.

Staring at Lakeview's impeccably shiny floor, I took a deep breath. "It's nothing. Or, I mean, I guess it is *something*. But . . . " I shook my head and reset. "It's just that I've been trying to find time to be with you for weeks! But every time I reach out, it's 'I can't, I'm having dinner with Buddy' or 'Oops, Buddy and I are going to the movies' or 'Sorry, but we're staring dreamily into each other's eyes for the next four hours.'"

"Ouch," Helen said. "I mean, I guess I haven't had a lot of free time lately. But I just started dating Buddy—so that's normal, isn't it? And I've had a million other things to do, like finals and practice."

"Sure," I said, closing my locker. "But you still have time to spend whispering with Bianca, right?"

Although I didn't mean it, my voice came out as acidic as vinegar.

Helen's eyes widened, and she just shook her head. "That's not fair," she said. "I'm allowed to have other friends."

"Right," I said. "I think you've made that abundantly clear. Anyways, thanks for asking if I'm okay," I told her. "It really helped."

And with that, I walked away.

Even as I stomped off down the hallway, I felt awful about what had just happened, my cheeks burning with shame. I thought about turning around and apologizing, but my pride forced me to keep walking. I climbed onto my bike, hoping that I'd feel better by the time I reached home. Instead, I felt worse. When I walked into my apartment, my chest swirled with anxiety so thick that each breath felt like I was half-submerged in water.

"You're home fast," Mrs. Lee said as I closed the door behind me. "Good day at school?"

Afraid that I'd tear up as soon as I started speaking, I just shook my head and rushed to my bedroom. But I hadn't taken my first step inside when my mouth dropped open.

My room was trashed.

My floor looked like an abstract painting of broken ornaments and shredded golden tinsel, and there was a huge wet spot in the middle of my rug.

My ears ringing, I rushed over to the side of my bed. That's where I had been storing Bianca's box of decorations—a box that was now absolutely destroyed.

For a moment, I just stared at the carnage, my eyes wide and unblinking, my arms wrapped around my torso like they were keeping me from falling apart. And then I screamed. I didn't know what had come over me. One minute, I was staring down at the ruined decorations, wondering how I was possibly going to pay Bianca back for all of it when I was already completely broke. The next moment, I was shouting at the top of my lungs.

Panting, I rushed into the living room, determined to find Boz. I didn't even know what I planned to do once I found him—I didn't think cats particularly cared if you yelled at them—but as I craned my neck around the living room, I couldn't spot him. Instead, my eyes zeroed in on something else entirely.

Mrs. Lee's tarot cards.

They were balanced on the edge of the coffee table in a neat little stack, and the sight of them made my breath catch in my throat. For a moment, all I could think about was the Tower card. The violent lightning and the desperate look in the couple's eyes as they leaped from the fiery inferno. Ever since Mrs. Lee's reading, everything had gone wrong.

She had predicted imminent catastrophe, and she had been right.

As if somebody flipped a switch in my brain, my anger at Boz dissolved into dejection, and before I could stop myself, tears spilled from the corners of my eyes and slipped down my cheeks. Soon, I was full-on sobbing in the middle of the living room.

"Oh dear," Mrs. Lee said. "What's wrong?"

"E-everything!" I hiccupped. "You were right! You predicted disaster, and that's exactly what happened! First with Marvel and Eliot, and then with the party, and then I was supposed to tell the Royals that we didn't have a place for it, but then I saw Helen and Buddy kissing and it freaked me out, and then B-boz ate the decorations—"

"Whoa there. Let's slow down," Mrs. Lee said. Taking off her giant glasses, she peered at me like an owl. "First, what do you mean, I was right?"

"About the Tower card!" I burst out. "Back at the laundromat, you predicted that my future would be miserable, and now it is!"

"*That's* what has you in this state?" Mrs. Lee raised her eyebrows.

In response, all I could do was wail, "*Yes!*"

Mrs. Lee shook her head and patted an empty spot on her mattress. I sank down next to her and buried my damp face in my hands. For a while, we just stayed there like that— me trying to muffle my sobs, and Mrs. Lee rubbing gentle circles on my back. It was only when the worst of my gasps had calmed that Mrs. Lee tilted my chin so that I was staring into her eyes.

"Listen closely, dear, because this is important," Mrs. Lee told me. "I sympathize with your struggles, but if you don't like the way your future is taking shape—then it's up to you to fix it."

"But the tarot cards said—"

"Never mind what the tarot cards said. Tarot is all about possibility," Mrs. Lee stressed. "The cards show you one path your future *may* take, but not necessarily the one it *will* take. Does that make sense?"

"I—I don't know." I sniffled.

As I swallowed down another bout of tears, Mrs. Lee squeezed my hand. "Everyone makes mistakes, love. Sometimes it's your fault, and sometimes it's not. But what's important to remember is that no matter what happens, your future can always be changed—only, you can't just wait around for that change to come. You have to be the one to take charge and do something about it. You don't give up."

Mrs. Lee rummaged through her purse for a tissue, and I mulled over her words. The future wasn't set in stone. The tarot cards didn't have the final say. Then did that mean I could still repair things?

No. There were only seven more days until Christmas Eve. I might be able to patch things up with Eliot and Marvel, but there was nothing I could do about the party. I'd have to tell the Royals about it. Then deal with the fallout. "Take charge," as Mrs. Lee said, and try to mend things with them afterward.

Another few tears leaked down my cheeks, and Mrs. Lee handed me a tissue from the packet in her purse. "Oh my," she sighed. "You really are in a state, aren't you? Come on." She made a beckoning gesture with her hand. "Tell me all about it."

Gradually, the whole sorry story came out. How I'd said I would host the party, just because Caroline thought I couldn't do it. How Mina had said no. (I didn't mention that she said no because of Mrs. Lee—that seemed too rude.) How I'd tried to find another place but it was too expensive. And the whole story of Helen and Buddy, and me and Marvel, and me and Eliot.

I stopped talking at last, and just sat there for a second, hiccupping and sniffling. Mrs. Lee handed me another tissue. As she tucked the packet back into her purse, something fell out with a metallic jingle. Mrs. Lee's apartment key.

I bent down, picked up the key, and tried to hand it back to her.

She started to take it. But then she closed her hand into a fist. "No," she said. "You hang on to that. You might want to use it."

For a moment, I didn't understand what she meant. Then I gasped as I got it.

"You mean..." I breathed. "You mean... I can have the party in your apartment?"

She nodded. "Exactly."

"But... that's a really, really big favor," I said.

Mrs. Lee waved her hand through the air. "It's not that big. After all, you three have been so kind to me, letting me stay here ... and besides, I trust you, Pippa, dear. I know your heart is always in the right place."

As Mrs. Lee gently folded my fingers around the key, I

had to stop myself from bursting into tears for the third time. Unable to speak, I lunged forward and gave her a hug.

Mrs. Lee squeezed me back, and then I sprinted upstairs.

I couldn't believe I had just solved one of my biggest problems.

Bouncing up and down with energy, I slipped the key into the hole, pulled open the door, flipped on the lights—and gasped.

20

CLEAN SLATE

Only 7 Days Until Christmas Eve

(Can I Do It All?)

I stared into Mrs. Lee's apartment, my mouth hanging open. And not in a good, "whoa, this is my dream party space" way either. More like, I was wondering how one woman could have *that* many cat pictures. There were at least a dozen different portraits of Boz hanging on the walls. And that wasn't all.

I slowly ventured farther into her dim apartment, my hands up in a defensive pose, prepared for something to jump out of the shadows and grab me. The next thing I noticed was that Mrs. Lee hadn't taken out the trash before she moved in with us. The place smelled like a revolting mixture of rotten bananas and spoiled milk. The third thing I noticed was that it was about negative ten degrees—colder than the ice room at a Korean spa. Mrs. Lee must have turned off the heat before leaving.

On top of that, the place was kind of a disaster: boxes full of old newspapers, racks of antiquated clothing, and a thousand knickknacks covering every surface. All in all, it wasn't exactly the kind of apartment I could see the Royals sipping mocktails in.

But one thing was for sure—it was better than no apartment.

I stared at the photos of Boz taken from twelve different angles, evaluating how much work I'd need to do over the next few days. I couldn't help but imagine Mrs. Lee up here, all alone on Christmas Eve, sipping lukewarm tea and humming carols to herself. My stomach twisted. Had I really been so desperate to get rid of her just a few weeks ago? I felt so bad about that now.

At that thought, I took a deep breath. Mrs. Lee had given me much more than her key tonight—she had also given me some excellent advice. For the past month, I'd had plenty of opportunities to tell Helen and Buddy about how I felt left out. But I hadn't. I had just buried my insecurities deeper and deeper until my feelings morphed into resentment. I had kept waiting for things to go back to normal, but I refused to take the initiative to make that happen.

Even if I managed to throw the world's best party, it would be an empty success if I didn't have my best friends partying with me. And so even though cleaning this space up was going to take almost all my free time, there was something more pressing I had to do right now.

I grabbed the dirty trash, carried it downstairs to the curb, then headed to my bedroom. Hugging a pillow to my chest, I sat cross-legged in bed and dialed first Helen's, then Buddy's number. My fingers shook as I pressed Conference.

Part of me sort of hoped that the call would go to voice mail, but for once, they both picked up.

"Hello?" they chorused—and I froze.

"Buddy? Is that you?" Helen asked, sounding confused.

"Uh . . . yup, I think so," Buddy replied.

After a long, uncomfortable silence, Helen asked, "Pippa? Are you there?"

"Yes," I managed to squeak out in a voice that sounded almost nothing like mine. I quickly cleared my throat. "Yes," I said again, firmer this time.

Another painfully long silence.

"Um, you did call us," Buddy finally said, sounding confused. "Right?"

"Right."

I swallowed hard. My throat felt drier than a dying cactus. I was ashamed of the way I had treated Helen earlier.

It was easier to feel anger than it was to feel sadness. It was easier to blame Helen and Buddy instead of accepting that sometimes things changed and you had to change with them. And I had no real idea how to articulate any of this to them over the phone, but I did know where to start.

"I called because . . . because I wanted to say that I am sorry," I said. "Especially to you, Helen. I was rude to you for no reason today. And I've been thinking about it nonstop—about how I lost my temper, and how it wasn't your fault that I've been keeping all my problems to myself. It wasn't fair of me to take that out on you."

"It did take me a little by surprise." Helen paused. "Although I could tell *something* was wrong. And you *were* mad at me, weren't you?"

"Well, no. Kind of. I don't know." I glanced down at my lap, trying to find the right way to word things. It felt so *embarrassing* to admit how insecure I had become. "Now that my head is clearer, I don't think I was mad at either of you," I finally said. "But I was definitely jealous."

"Jealous?" Buddy spluttered. Even though I couldn't see him, I could picture the rapid-fire way he would be blinking right now.

"Well, yeah. I was jealous that the two of you were spending so much time together—and not with me."

Before either of them could react, I quickly added, "And I know that I'm not your only friend, and that you're allowed to hang out with each other however much you want, and I can't force you to do anything. I *know* that." I sucked in a huge gulp of breath. "But I couldn't help but think you didn't like me as much, now that you had each other. I guess I was just scared that you two were leaving me behind. Which sucked, because you two are my favorite people, and I've missed you so much."

Finally, I stopped to give them a chance to speak. As I waited for a reply, I felt a mixture of trepidation and relief. I didn't know what they would say, but at least I had said my part.

After a long silence, Buddy finally cleared his throat. "I'm sorry, Pippa," he said. It was one of the few times I had heard him use my first name. "I didn't know you felt that way. But it makes sense. I mean, I know exactly what it feels like to be on the other side of that equation," he said pointedly. "But really, I wasn't ignoring you. Though now I see I kind of did."

"Same," Helen said. "Only . . . you honestly thought I didn't like you anymore?" Her voice was so shocked that it made the mere idea seem silly.

I breathed in, and for the first time in a week, it felt easy.

"Aw, Pips, I'm sorry," she went on. "I didn't mean to make you feel that way. Buddy is my boyfriend, but you're still my best friend. And that's not going to change, no matter what happens!"

228

I wanted to ask Helen what she and Bianca had been whispering about, but this definitely didn't seem like the right time for that.

"Ditto, Park," Buddy picked up where Helen had left off. "I mean, I love being with Helen. But I *also* love telling you all about it! And just because I have a girlfriend doesn't mean I can't still have a best bud for basketball and crappy movies and stuff like that."

Their words felt like a warm blanket nestled over my shoulders. After nearly three weeks of feeling like *less* than second choice, I finally realized how silly I had been, keeping everything to myself.

"I love you guys," I said, my throat thick, my eyes filling with tears.

"And we love you," Helen said.

"So . . . is everything okay, now?" Buddy asked.

"Yes," I said. Then I swallowed. "Well, sort of."

"Sort of?" Helen repeated carefully.

I was *really* glad we were having this conversation over the phone—no one could see how blazing red my face had just turned.

"So," I said. "You know how the Christmas party is seven days from now?"

"Yes," Buddy and Helen answered.

"Right," I said. "Okay. First off, let me say that I *do* have

229

a space to hold the party. Now. But it's not my apartment. And the place is kind of a wreck. And Boz destroyed all the decorations."

"Boz?" Helen asked.

"That's Mrs. Lee's cat," I explained. "Mrs. Lee is the lady sleeping in our living room."

Then I told them everything. How Mrs. Lee had broken her leg after I had already committed to throwing the party. How I had tried so hard to secure a new venue. How close I had come to confessing so many different times . . .

After I finished, I stared at my phone's screen and held my breath, waiting for them to say something.

"Wow." Buddy broke the silence. "Not going to lie, Park. That was *a lot*."

"I know," I groaned. "But like I said, I do have a place to throw the party. Mrs. Lee is letting me use her apartment upstairs. It's, uh, on the shabby side. And right now it's a little crammed . . . and chilly . . . and maybe a little smelly. . . . But I know I can get it to work."

"That's great," Helen said. "But when are you going to tell the other Royals?"

My mouth scrunched up like I was chewing on a lemon. "Soon?"

"Just tell them, Pips," Helen said. "Everything will be okay. This party was never meant to be a competition. You have to learn to ignore Caroline." She laughed. "Instead, think about it like when we're all on the court together, practicing for the big game! A party like this needs *teamwork*."

She was right. I *knew* she was right. But I still clutched my pillow tighter to my chest, and I couldn't stop the spasm of fear that rocked through me. Telling the rest of the Royals about what I had done was still going to be hard—really hard—but I knew one thing. It was going to be a lot easier with my friend Helen by my side.

. . .

I arranged an emergency meeting with the Royals at Duo's after school the next day. I could have done it at lunch, but I didn't want to spoil the last day of school. Also, there was a decent chance Caroline was going to scream at me, and if that happened, I didn't want it to be in the middle of the Lakeview cafeteria.

Helen and I arrived at Duo's early and grabbed a booth in the back. At the sight of Win, Bianca, Starsie, and Caroline strutting across the threshold, my heart leaped into my throat, and I briefly wondered if twelve-year-olds could get heart attacks.

"Don't forget to breathe, Pips." Helen squeezed my hand. "You're turning a little blue."

Right. I forced myself to inhale and exhale.

Even in basketball shorts, the Royals intimidated me, but today, they looked like a force to be reckoned with. Caroline and Bianca wore matching black North Face jackets, and Win and Starsie had their golden Royals scrunchies bobbing in their high ponytails. As they headed our way, Starsie said something funny, and they laughed, white teeth gleaming from all the way across the diner. Seeing them like this reminded me of why I had been so desperate to impress them in the first place. They looked . . . well . . . like royalty.

"Hey, Helen! Hi, Pippa!" Starsie said.

She slid into a seat next to me and squeezed my shoulder. But when Bianca, all business, said, "So, what's with the meeting?" I had to fight the urge to push Starsie out of my way and sprint straight out of Duo's, all the way home. It was only Helen's reminder—*this party was never meant to be a competition*—that kept me glued to my seat.

"Well?" Caroline pressed.

I took a deep breath . . . and then I stopped procrastinating. "Okay, right. So, the thing is . . . "

I didn't look anyone in the face as I explained what had happened. Instead, I stared straight down at the melting marshmallows in my cocoa cup and acted like the rest of them couldn't even hear me.

After I had finished telling them everything, I finally looked up. "I really did want to throw the ultimate party," I said, willing them to believe me. "And I think that's why I messed up so badly. I kept thinking that if I just *wanted* it hard enough, I could fix everything. And instead, I let you all down."

I lowered my gaze, too afraid to see the judgment in their eyes. For a while, nobody said anything.

Caroline was the first person to break the silence.

"You're right about one thing," she said, her voice steely. "You *did* let us all down."

Although I had been expecting it, I still flinched. But then something I definitely didn't expect happened. "Ouch." Starsie winced. "C, that was, like, *way* harsh."

"Yeah," Win agreed. "You've been so aggressive lately. I mean, on the court it's fine. But off the court, it's just plain mean."

Caroline's eyebrows shot up. Clearly, she had expected the rest of the Royals to be on her side.

"Well, excuse me for being a little upset," she huffed. "But we've been planning this party for a month now! And Pippa ruined it! She ruined *everything*!"

"Now you're just being a drama queen," Win said in her usual calm, sensible voice. "Pippa told us she found a new place to hold the party. And it's in the same apartment building. We don't even have to switch addresses."

"I'm being *a drama queen*?" Caroline ignored everything else Win had said. "We throw this party every year, Winona."

233

"Since last year," Helen pointed out, but Caroline ranted on without stopping.

"It's *our* thing. The Royal brand. It's supposed to represent us! So what will everyone think when they show up to some random one-room apartment?" Caroline's voice started to rise, and I tried not to shrink back in my seat. "Besides, you heard her! The dumb cat messed up the decorations, too!"

Helen and Starsie both tried to cut in, but Caroline wouldn't let them. She was more furious than I had ever seen her, and somehow, I didn't think it was solely because of the party. Caroline had always been snarky toward me. I just wished I knew *why*.

"Ugh!" Caroline shook her head and glared at me. "I just don't understand why the rest of you are so *obsessed* with Pippa that you can't see what a total disaster this is! In fact—"

But just as Caroline's voice started to reach a pitch high enough to break glass, someone else broke in.

"I mean this respectfully, Caroline . . . but will you *please* shut up?"

Everyone at the table sucked in a breath, including Caroline. Because it wasn't Win or Helen or even Starsie who had said that.

It was Bianca. And based on the look in her eyes, she wasn't finished.

"Everyone has problems," Bianca snapped. "All of us.

But your problems are just . . . they're so trivial. And this is coming from someone who's your friend, C! But you've been going on and on about this stupid party for weeks now like it's the freaking apocalypse or something, when *some* of us are dealing with actual issues."

At this, Bianca's voice warbled slightly—something that I had never heard happen before. Without warning, a single tear slid down her perfectly smooth cheek. She wiped it away immediately, but not before the rest of us could see.

"Bianca?" Win said tentatively. "Are you . . . okay?"

For a moment, Bianca's eyes flared with her signature aloofness before cooling into something like indecision. Breathing in sharply, she seemed to make a snap decision.

"Not really," she said. She drew a shaky breath. "My parents are getting divorced."

The table went silent. My mouth popped open, and across the table, I saw Caroline's jaw drop. Clearly, she'd had no idea, either. I glanced at Helen to see how she was taking the news, but she just nodded at Bianca encouragingly.

At that, the memory of Helen and Bianca whispering in the locker room flashed through my mind. I had assumed the two were gossiping about me. But now I was pretty sure that had been the furthest thing from the truth. I felt a rush of guilt mixed with relief.

"I'm so sorry, B," Starsie said. "That's awful!"

"Yeah, well, I'm not trying to get anyone's pity or anything," Bianca said, her voice gruff and a little embarrassed. But at the same time, she seemed relieved to have her secret out in the open. "I'm just saying, there are worse things than having a party-space problem, Caroline, okay?"

"Okay," Caroline said. And for once, she didn't have anything snarky to add. She just sat there, looking confused and a little hurt.

"Now, back to the party," Bianca said. She cleared her throat, and just like that, the vulnerable, open Bianca was gone, replaced by the regal Ice Queen I was used to. "We have a place. We need new decorations. Is there anything else you haven't told us?"

"Um . . . there is one other thing," I admitted. "I know everyone's expecting some fancy catering situation, but I don't have the money for that. But don't worry! I'm going to ask Jung-Hwa to cook, and he makes Korean food so good, you'll swear you're at a fancy restaurant!"

I scanned the Royals' faces, trying to see what they thought about this, but mostly they just looked confused. Not exactly the reaction I had expected.

"Wait, wait, wait." Win shook her head, her ponytail bobbing along with the motion. "Korean food sounds great . . . but what do you mean, you can't afford the catering? We never expected you to do that!"

Now it was my turn to be confused. "What do you mean?"

"We all chip in for the food," Starsie answered. "You were just supposed to pick the restaurant and put in the order. Didn't Caroline tell you that?"

My gaze darted to Caroline. She sank lower in her seat, her nostrils flaring, and her eyes lowered. "I thought I did," she muttered. And maybe the Pippa of yesterday would have called her on it, but today, I was feeling generous.

"Oh," I said. "Caroline told me so many details about the party, I must have missed that one. It was a pretty big detail for me to miss . . . but I'm so relieved to hear it." I gave Caroline a knowing glance.

She looked at me, her eyes wide and her mouth scrunched up—like she was both grateful to me *and* resentful at the same time. Honestly, I had no idea how that was even possible. Of course, there was a lot I didn't know about Caroline. And maybe someday in the future I'd find out more about her—like why she hated me so much.

But for now, I had better, happier things to focus on. For the first time in a long time, the future seemed bright.

After one more unpleasant but very necessary chore, that is: I had to apologize to Marvel.

21

A VERY PIPPA PAGEANT

Only 1 Day Until Christmas Eve

(And I'm Finally Ready!)

"Places, everyone!" Pastor Oh called. "It's nearly time!"

After all those rehearsals, it was hard to believe that the big night was finally here. I gathered my sheep posse at the front of the stage and reminded them to stay quiet until the curtain rose, but they could barely stand still. I think I was as nervous as they were—though for a different reason.

I'd gone to the pageant dress rehearsal on Sunday with butterflies in my stomach, ready to throw myself at Marvel's feet. However, his feet were not in evidence. I mean, he never showed up. At a break, I asked Pastor Oh where he was.

"Poor boy, he wasn't feeling well," Pastor Oh said. "I hope he'll be better in time for the show! But even if he's not, I have confidence that you can hold the show together, Pippa."

"Thanks," I said, trying to sound like I meant it. Part of me was relieved that I didn't have to face Marvel yet, but the other part of me wished I could see him and just get it over with. And another part of me just wanted to *see* him, with his messy hair and his ever-present headphones.

Now it was showtime, and Marvel was here but doing an excellent job of avoiding me. When I was onstage, he made sure he was backstage. When I was backstage, he was out front, checking the lighting. He seemed to know exactly where I'd be and made sure that's exactly where he wasn't. And somehow, he had gotten out of being a shepherd onstage during the performance.

I was sure it was because of me.

Trying to shake that thought away, I focused on nicer things. Like how I had spent the last five hours with Buddy and Helen in Mrs. Lee's apartment. Even though we were only cleaning, I had more fun than I'd had in weeks.

"It's starting!" Annie whispered, interrupting my wandering thoughts.

The house lights went down and the audience grew quiet.

The kids murmured in excitement, and even my own stomach did a little backflip. Unable to resist, I sneaked a glance around the rising curtain. My eyebrows shot up. There were way more people in the audience than I had expected. Not an empty seat anywhere!

I searched for Mina and Jung-Hwa in the crowd, but before I could spot them, Peter stepped out onto the stage, and I quickly ducked back behind the curtain.

"Our story begins a long, long time ago," he announced. "We start with a woman called Mary . . . "

The next hour passed in a blur. Before tonight, we hadn't made it through a single rehearsal without at least three kids forgetting their lines. But tonight, no one messed up—a true Christmas miracle. A couple of the angels did lose their wings, and one of the Wise Men tripped over a cow. We weren't perfect. But when the whole cast emerged for the grand finale, the audience erupted in cheers. Especially Jung-Hwa. Even though he was sitting in the back, I could hear him yelling, "Go, Pippa!" all the way up on the stage.

After the cast took three consecutive bows, Pastor Oh climbed up on the stage with his wife. He was in his usual religious attire, but Mrs. Oh was dressed like she was going to meet the president or something. She looked like a princess in her ice-blue gown, with her black hair braided in a crown around her head.

"Now, wasn't that an *amazing* way to celebrate Christmas?" Pastor Oh asked the audience. His face was ruddy red with happiness. "I'm so proud of all the hard work that these children have put into this performance, and I am very grateful that so many of you have come out to show your support."

As the audience started to clap again, I caught a slight movement from the opposite side of the stage. I locked eyes with Marvel; then he ducked out of sight. My heart lurched.

"Before we wrap things up here, I want to extend my sincerest gratitude to a few people in particular," Pastor Oh announced, and I tried to focus on his words to distract myself from the sinking feeling in my stomach. "First, a huge thank you to Mr. Marvel Moon. Marvel was the first volunteer to sign on with the pageant, and when he wasn't hiding backstage, listening to music, he was very helpful and always put a smile on our faces."

Pastor Oh paused to let the audience laugh before continuing. "Next, I need to extend my sincerest gratitude to Ms. Pippa Park. In addition to being a positive role model for the other children, without Pippa, this pageant might have never happened! You see, every great performance takes hard work and patience, but last week, when that patience started to run thin, Pippa stepped up and reminded us that we were all team players. We were all in this together!"

Pastor Oh turned so that his eyes met mine, and I looked down with a blush.

"Before I let you go, I wanted to give one last shout-out," Pastor Oh declared. "This time to our very own parish member, Ms. Mina Kim. Ms. Kim owns the Lucky Laundromat, and she has graciously partnered with the church to help wash the costumes after tonight's performance. I can't recommend her services enough—and in exciting news, starting now and leading up to Seollal, we'll have a box in the parish to drop off receipts from Lucky's. When you drop one off, you'll automatically be entered into our Lunar New Year's raffle—and you really don't want to miss this year's prize: a brand-new kimchi fridge!"

At this, the audience let out an even bigger cheer. I couldn't see my family from here, but I had a feeling Jung-Hwa was hanging onto Mina and going wild. As Pastor Oh finished his speech, I led the kids to the dressing room, and we all changed. Then I headed out to find Mina and Jung-Hwa.

Halfway there, I spotted Marvel slipping through a side door.

Now or never. I dashed after him.

When I caught up to him, I grabbed his shoulder, and he twisted around, surprised.

"Pippa!" He blinked. For a brief moment, his eyes were wide and vulnerable. Then he shook his head, and they seemed to harden. He took a step back. "What do you want?"

His voice didn't sound as angry as I had expected—more wary. But the emotional distance between us made my chest ache. I shifted from one foot to the other, trying to decide how to answer his question. I knew I had hurt him pretty badly. And if he never wanted to talk to me again, then really, there was nothing I could do to change that. But I had to at least try to make things right. And at the very least, I needed to say one thing.

"I'm sorry," I said. "I know canceling our date to hang out with someone else was selfish and wrong of me. And I really did like you! Do, I mean! A lot." My voice dropped lower. "But, well, I was still kind of crushing on this other guy when I met you, and I was trying to get over it because I didn't think he liked me back . . . but then it turned out that he maybe did, and, oh, I don't know . . . it's not even that I liked him more than you, it's just that I was so *used* to wanting him. . . . "

I shook my head, feeling like I was doing everything wrong. I wanted Marvel to understand that I hadn't hurt him on purpose, but I didn't know if talking about Eliot was a good idea. And Marvel's expression definitely wasn't helping. His eyes were as hard as flint and as unreadable, too.

"Anyways." I took a deep breath. "That stuff doesn't matter. The thing is, I shouldn't have canceled on you, no matter what the reason. It was terrible of me. I know we don't really see each other outside of rehearsals, so if you don't want to see me again, then you don't have to. Obviously. But I wanted to let you know that no matter what you think, I really don't have a boyfriend. And I'd still really like it if you came to my party. So . . . um, yeah," I said, running out of steam. "It's tomorrow afternoon at one, if you decide to come."

I waited for Marvel to say something, but he just shrugged. Since there was nothing more for me to add, I just swallowed.

"Right. Well, I guess I'll see you around," I said. "Or not."

And because every second I stood in front of Marvel felt like I was standing on burning coals, I made my escape.

He hadn't responded exactly how I had wanted him to. He hadn't thrown his arms around me or confessed his undying love. Well, I guess I hadn't *really* expected that. But still . . . it would have been nice. . . .

Oh well. At least I had told him everything that was on my mind—with a hundred-percent honesty.

And as I rejoined my family, the weight on my shoulders was finally gone.

22

A PERFECT
PIPPA PARK PARTY

Christmas Eve (And All's Well!)

"Five minutes until one, girls," Bianca announced.
"Everyone ready?"

"Almost," Win said. "I just can't get this bowtie
clipped."

"And I need one last coat of lip-gloss," Caroline added,
popping open her purse.

As Helen helped Win fasten her green-and-red bowtie, and Caroline tested out different lip-gloss flavors in the
bathroom, I smoothed my hands down the silky fabric of my
dress and tucked a tendril of hair back into the fancy updo
Mrs. Lee had helped me with. It was hard to believe that after
a month of sweating about this party, the big day was finally
here. A spike of nerves shot through me, and I gazed around

Mrs. Lee's apartment, searching for any last-minute improvements before the party officially began.

I couldn't find one thing I'd change—which was honestly impressive, considering that three days ago, not even Marie Kondo could have salvaged this place. But with the help of Helen and Buddy, all the old newspapers had been boxed and stored under Mrs. Lee's bed, it smelled like the Vanilla Sugar Cookie candle flickering on the coffee table, and we had a space heater in the corner that warmed up the room nicely. The numerous photo albums showcasing Boz had been carefully tucked away, and it was Buddy's idea to tape tiny Santa hats on the photos on the walls.

But that wasn't all. Although Bianca's decorations were beyond saving, she and Mina had teamed up to make new ones. Now, a cascade of silver paper snowflakes drifted down from the ceiling on invisible threads, and a dozen different pillows with golden velour pillowcases dotted the living room, giving the impression that the floor was made of plushy gold.

But what was happening in the kitchen was the best part of all.

I peeked in, and my stomach rumbled at the sight of the feast waiting for us on the Formica countertops. Since the catering businesses in town were already booked by the time we tried to find one, the Royals had all pitched in for grocery money, and Jung-Hwa had gone to *town*. There were crispy kimchi pancakes, savory *dongtaejeon*, and enough Korean fried chicken to feed the entire girls' basketball team—and we could eat *a lot*. That alone would have been enough reason to salivate, but the make-your-own *bibimbap* bar was my favorite by far. Jung-Hwa had made a huge batch of white rice and set out all the necessary accoutrements—bowls of bean sprouts, fernbrake, carrots, shiitake mushrooms, and spinach in sesame oil, along with a huge vat of vivid red bibimbap sauce on the side. Win and Helen had baked two cakes, and Bianca had brought some sugar cookies and gingerbread men that she'd made with her mom.

"I know what you're thinking, Park, but fair warning: I'm pretty sure your friends would *kill* you if you mess up that spread before they snap any pics."

I glanced over at Buddy and laughed. "You're probably right."

Still, I sneaked a chicken wing when he wasn't looking.

The doorbell rang just as I finished wiping the sauce from my mouth. As the first few Lakeview kids trickled in, I anxiously watched their expressions, searching for a sign that my party setup didn't measure up to the previous Royals' party. But all I could see were smiling faces and lots of hugging.

"Mmm! It smells so good in here!" one girl exclaimed as another one oohed and aahed over the paper snowflakes.

At the sound of their voices, Caroline hurried out of the bathroom, ready to play the glamorous host. And although I was used to seeing this side of Bianca, this was the first opportunity I had to see her shine.

"Welcome, everyone!" she said, her voice sweet but somehow still commanding. "Long time no see, Richie! I *love* your dress, Venus. And Jackie—that purse! Is it vintage?"

She sashayed from guest to guest in her golden A-line dress, laughing, tossing around compliments, and basking in their praise. It was a facet of Bianca that I didn't see on the basketball court or in class, and it was another equally impressive side of her.

As more kids arrived, I headed over to Buddy and Helen, glad to leave the social side of hosting to Bianca and Caroline. They were both grooving out to a playlist Win had made, and within a few minutes, they weren't the only ones. I hadn't come up with any special entertainment, but nobody seemed to mind.

Still, despite the fact that everyone looked like they were having fun, there was an uneasy fluttering feeling in my stomach that wouldn't go away. As the clock ticked past two, my eyes kept darting to the front door.

I hadn't heard anything from Marvel, but that didn't stop me from hoping it would be him every time the doorbell rang. I glanced down at my dress and sighed. It was the most luxurious thing I had ever worn. Wouldn't it be a shame if nobody special saw me in it?

" . . . and that's how Pippa's long-lost grandmother swam across the Pacific Ocean. But wait until you hear how the dolphins helped her. It's hilarious. Right, Park?"

"Right," I mumbled. Then I did a double take. "Wait, what?"

Buddy and Helen giggled.

"See?" Buddy said. "I told you she's not listening!"

"Yeah, she's too busy checking out the front door," Helen said. "Waiting for somebody special."

My cheeks flushed. Trying to maintain some dignity, I straightened my shoulders and held my chin high. "What? No way! I am *not* waiting for anybody! Everyone who matters is here."

"Aww, Pips! That's so sweet," Helen said. "So you really don't care who just walked in?"

I whipped around and watched as Eliot pushed through the crowd, scanning the room. He met my shocked gaze and gave a small wave. As he made his way toward us, I smiled at him, but internally I was freaking out. And not just because he looked mind-scramblingly good. I was used to seeing him in his Lakeview uniform, but tonight he wore a pair of dark jeans and a striped button-down shirt, and his hair was a little damp from the rain outside, and—*that is so not the point,* I reminded myself. I hadn't spoken to him since our not-quite-a-date at the mall. I had estimated there was about a zero-point-five percent chance of him showing up tonight. Much less to be headed my way. . . .

"Hey, Pippa. Hi, Helen." Eliot nodded at us.

"Eliot! Good to see you," Helen said casually.

I wanted to be casual, too. But I was pretty sure if I spoke right now my voice would come out as a high-pitched shriek. So, to keep it safe, I simply bobbed my head.

There was an awkward moment of silence, and then Eliot whistled. "Wow," he said, glancing around Mrs. Lee's apartment. "You did a great job with the decorations, Pippa."

"Oh, well, it wasn't just me," I said, finally finding my voice. "I mean, I had a lot of help from my family, and trust me, without Helen and Buddy, this place would still look like something from *Hoarders.*"

Helen and Buddy laughed, but Eliot stiffened a little.

"Buddy?" he asked.

"Present!"

Buddy set down one of the kimchi pancakes he was munching on and wiped the excess grease on his pants before sticking his hand out. Eliot gazed down at it like he'd been offered a dead fish.

"Buddy's one of my oldest friends," I explained. "He's also Helen's boyfriend."

"Helen's . . . boyfriend?" Eliot repeated.

As his eyes widened, someone coughed behind me. I turned—and nearly choked on my own spit.

"Marvel!" I said.

He was standing only a foot away, looking adorably nervous in a dark hoodie with his best pair of jeans.

"That's me," he said.

"You came!"

"Yeah, well, you know me. I couldn't let your party flop."

Marvel's words were teasing, but his expression still looked a little uncertain. His gaze darted between me and Eliot, like he was wondering if he had made a big mistake coming. But before he could change his mind and leave, I grabbed him by the sleeve and tugged him closer.

"I'm so glad you made it. Everyone, meet Marvel," I said. "He's a . . . a friend from church. And, Marvel, meet everyone. I mean, you kind of already met Eliot. But this is my best friend, Helen, and my other best friend, Buddy."

"Ah, so this is Buddy," Marvel said. I was relieved that his tone was warming up, even if his gaze was still wary. "I've heard a lot about you."

"Yeah? All good things, I hope!" Buddy said.

Marvel gave a strange smile, but before he could reply, "All I Want for Christmas Is You" came on, and Helen squealed.

"I love this one! Dance with me, Buddy?" She grabbed his hand and led him to the center of the room.

Spending time with Eliot or Marvel one-on-one was exciting, but having them both here? I gulped. Without Helen and Buddy as a buffer, I had no idea what to say. Eliot liked to talk math and grades, but Marvel had never shown any interest in that. And Marvel enjoyed bad puns and K-pop music, but Eliot probably didn't even know who BLACKPINK were.

But before I could figure out what to do, someone called out, "Oh, there you are, Pippa!"

I recognized Bianca's sugary-sweet, *Eliot-is-within-hearing-range* voice. But this time, instead of setting my teeth on edge, I actually felt a shiver of relief.

"Oh, and Eliot! You made it—I didn't even see you come in." She twirled a brown curl around her finger and batted her long eyelashes at him.

"Um, yeah." Eliot shrugged. "I said I would."

"Well, we're *more* than happy to have you."

When Eliot just smiled, she glanced over at Marvel. "And who is this? Wait, no, don't tell me—Marvel, right? Pippa's told us so much about you!"

Bianca flashed her gracious-host smile at him, and for a moment, my back muscles stiffened. I didn't want Bianca giving anyone the idea that Marvel and I were a couple. It was way too soon for that.

"I spotted one of your friends in the kitchen, and he looked a little lonely." Bianca looped her arm through Eliot's. "Plus, you *have* to try these watermelon popsicles Pippa's uncle brought. Caroline's on this forever-diet thing, and even she's had three tonight."

"Oh," Eliot blinked. "Um, sure, I guess."

He turned toward me and opened his mouth like he wanted to say something. Before he had the chance, Bianca tugged him away. I waited for the usual Bianca-Eliot angst to hit me, but my reaction surprised me. I still had a lot of complicated feelings for Eliot—feelings that I knew weren't going to be resolved overnight. But right now, I was just happy to be here with Marvel.

"Wow," Marvel said once the two of them were out of our hearing range. "I think she just became my favorite person."

I laughed. "Seriously, I want you to know that I didn't invite Eliot here as my date or anything tonight. He just came because we're friends."

"Well, I don't think *he* wants to be just friends," Marvel said. "And I could argue that point all day and night, only right now, I'd rather dance."

"With me?" I blurted. My heart was so light I thought it was about to lift out of my chest, and I was sure my cheeks were the same color as the bibimbap sauce.

He arched his eyebrows at me. "No, with the picture of that cat on the wall." He gave it a closer look. "Who is that, anyway? It looks evil."

"That's Boz," I told him. "You should meet him." I came to a sudden decision. "In fact, I think you should meet him right now. Along with some other people."

"What, before we dance?"

"Yes." I grabbed Marvel's hand and tugged him toward the door. "It'll just take a minute. Come on."

. . .

Five minutes later, we were back at the door of Mrs. Lee's apartment. I opened it as Marvel, Mina, and Jung-Hwa puffed up the stairs behind me. They were carrying Mrs. Lee between them, perched like a princess on a wobbly swivel chair. She wore a red-and-white Santa hat and a necklace of miniature Christmas-tree lights.

"Hello, darlings!" she shouted as they rolled her through the doorway. "Have no fear—Mrs. Lee is here!"

Marvel let go of the chair and put his hands on his knees, gasping. "I don't have the strength to dance anymore," he told me. "In fact, I may die right now."

"I'm on top of the world!" Mrs. Lee crowed as Jung-Hwa gently spun her around.

"Don't know about that." He smiled as he and Mina turned to go. "We'll be back in an hour to get you."

"Hear that, everyone? You get one hour of my time! Let's make the most of it!" Mrs. Lee shouted. She shook her arms in the air. "Now, who's ready to get funky?"

Once upon a time, I'm sure that would have embarrassed me so much I would have dropped out of school and entered the witness protection program. But today, I was just happy to be able to celebrate with Mrs. Lee—the woman who had made this all possible.

Mrs. Lee used one leg to roll herself around the room, stopping to chat with groups of kids as she went. A few of them seemed a little puzzled by her, but most were laughing at her jokes within a few seconds.

At last she rolled over to me and Marvel. "Well, dearie, color me impressed. This place hasn't been so dolled up since the eighties. And I'm keeping those hats on Boz all year round!"

I laughed. "I'm so glad we got you up here!"

Mrs. Lee tossed her head. "Oh, of course. You know me—I'd never miss a party!" Her eyes shone with joy.

"All right, everyone!" She clapped her hands together. Then she reached into her purse and whipped out a familiar black box. "Pippa's special entertainment has arrived! Who's ready for a holiday tarot reading?"

23

ROYAL

-1 Day Until Christmas Eve

(Can We Do It All Again?)

"Dinner in five!" Mina called. "Are you two almost ready?"

"Almost!" I shouted.

There was still one thing Mrs. Lee and I had to do before the Christmas festivities could truly start.

"Paint?" I asked.

"Check!"

"Superglue?"

"Here!"

"Flashlight?"

"On!"

While Mrs. Lee restrained Boz, I carefully squeezed a pea-sized dollop of superglue onto mini-me's neck. I held the head and the neck together for ten seconds, then blew on the figurine to help the glue set.

"Well?" Mrs. Lee craned her head closer to me. "How's it looking?"

I studied mini-me with a critical eye. Although there was still a slight scar from where Boz had nibbled at it, and the paint we had used to repair the chips on my hair was a shade too light, I hugged it close to my heart anyway.

"Better than ever," I declared.

Mrs. Lee squeezed my hand. "Well, let's put her back where she belongs, then."

I had just finished setting mini-me in her usual spot in the manger scene when Jung-Hwa announced that dinner was ready.

There was a steaming-hot plate of *bulgogi*, freshly made *japchae*, tangy kimchi, and enough fluffy white rice to drown in—not to mention a huge bowl of buttery mashed potatoes and canned apple sauce on the side. Personally, I had never understood the appeal of the apple sauce, but Jung-Hwa had read *A Christmas Carol* so many times by this point in his life that it was nonnegotiable.

As the four of us settled into our spots at the kitchen table, Jung-Hwa squeezed Mina's hand and mine and smiled. All of us had our problems—our good days and bad—but tonight, I think we were just grateful to have one another.

An hour later, we were stuffed from our heads to our toes. As Mrs. Lee fiddled with the top button on her pants, I looked over the array of sweet buns that Jung-Hwa had picked up from our favorite Korean bakery. They looked absolutely delicious, but not even I had room to fit one more bite into my mouth. Instead, we left the dishes in the sink for later and headed into the living room together.

As Boz curled up underneath our Charlie Brown–sized Christmas tree, Jung-Hwa, Mina, and I sat on the couch and dialed Omma's number. Technically, it was already the twenty-sixth in Korea, but that didn't matter. Christmas wouldn't be Christmas without hearing Omma's voice. And even though it was early morning there, Omma's voice was full of cheer.

"Keuriseumaseu jal bonaeseyo," she sang.

I smiled. Tears filled my eyes and a rush of warmth flooded my heart. "Merry Christmas to you, too, Omma!"

"How was your Christmas?" Mina asked. "Are you feeling all right?"

Omma started to answer, but before she could finish, there was a rap at the door.

"Are we expecting anyone?" Jung-Hwa asked Mina.

"Not that I recall . . . "

I shrugged. "Probably just a neighbor who needs something," I said. "I'll get it."

I jogged to the door, wondering who needed to borrow what. But when I swung it open, I was totally surprised.

"Helen!" I exclaimed. "And Bianca!"

"Merry Christmas!" they sang out.

The two of them were standing in my hallway in matching Christmas sweaters. Helen's smile stretched across her face, and even Bianca looked happy. My gaze darted back and forth between them.

"What are you two doing here?"

"It's Christmas," Bianca replied, in a tone that screamed *duh*. "And what's Christmas without a little present?"

"A present?" I repeated. "For me?" Immediately, my cheeks took on a pink tinge. After spending so much time and money on the party, I hadn't even thought about buying presents for the Royals. . . .

"It's just a small something," Helen reassured me. "We thought about giving it to you yesterday, but Bianca and I agreed to wait for Christmas. B, do you have the box?"

"One sec."

As Helen squeezed my shoulder, Bianca rummaged in her purse and brought out a tiny black box wrapped in a single red ribbon. It was so small I couldn't imagine what was inside.

I held my breath as I carefully tugged off the ribbon, opened the lid—and gasped. It was a golden scrunchie.

"For . . . me?" I whispered.

I held the hair tie up to the light, admiring the way it sparkled and gleamed. It was just a small strip of fabric, identical to the scrunchies every other Royal owned—but to me, it

259

was priceless. Unable to resist, I quickly pulled my hair into a bun at the crown of my head, beaming.

"Well?" Bianca asked, smiling. "How does it feel?"

A hard question, because it felt like a lot of things. Like belonging, and relief, and friendship. Like coming home from a long day and knowing the people you loved were waiting there for you.

"It feels . . . amazing!" I declared.

PIPPA PARK
CRUSH AT FIRST SIGHT

Bonus Content

Discussion Questions for Your Book Club

Q&A with Author Erin Yun

Glossary of Korean Words

Discussion Questions for Your Book Club

1. Discuss a specific scene that reveals Pippa's strong need to belong. How does Pippa feel caught between two worlds? Describe the two worlds in which she lives and explain how these two worlds create conflict within Pippa. How does Pippa's need for acceptance affect everything she does in school and outside of school?

2. Each year, the Royals have a Christmas Eve party. They wear fancy dresses, serve expensive food, and use extravagant decorations. Why do they think this is the most important social event of the year? How does Pippa become the host for this year's party? Why is it so important to Pippa that this party be a success? How might the Royals' idea of a great party change after Pippa's party?

3. Describe Caroline. Why does she get so much pleasure from insulting Pippa? What does this reveal about her character? Debate whether she is jealous of Pippa's athletic ability or prejudiced against Pippa's culture and her socioeconomic standing. The other Royals know that Caroline is the "mean girl." Why don't they do more to defend Pippa? How do they eventually come to Pippa's rescue?

4. Mrs. Lee is learning to read tarot cards and offers to read Pippa's and Buddy's cards. A three-card reading includes

a person's past, present, and future. Pippa draws cards that clearly represent her past and present. Why isn't Pippa sure she wants to know her future? Describe how the characters' attitudes toward the cards vary.

5. Helen is dating Buddy, Pippa's best friend from Victoria Middle School. Why does their relationship make Pippa feel odd? Why does Pippa leave Buddy's Hanukkah party? Explain what happens when Pippa reveals her feelings to Buddy and Helen.

6. The Korean Baptist Church is having a Christmas pageant, and Mina suggests that Pippa offer to help. What is Pippa's reaction to this suggestion? What does Mina gain from Pippa's participation? What is the source of Mina's stress? How does she expect Pippa to be understanding of the family's financial situation? Debate whether she expects too much of Pippa.

7. Pippa meets Marvel Moon at the first pageant rehearsal. What do they like about each other? How is this different from Pippa's relationship with Eliot? Later, Marvel sees a text that Pippa receives from Buddy and misinterprets it. How does this threaten Pippa and Marvel's relationship?

8. Discuss the crush Pippa has on Eliot. At what point does Eliot finally express his feelings for Pippa? Explain how Pippa's budding relationship with Eliot complicates matters with Marvel. Discuss the courage it takes to tell

Marvel everything with one-hundred-percent honesty. How does being honest and open give Pippa a feeling of relief?

9. Pippa needs to tell someone that the party is in jeopardy. Why is she confident that she can tell her troubles to Mrs. Lee? How does she blame Mrs. Lee for her problems? Discuss how Mrs. Lee helps Pippa accept responsibility for her own fate.

10. Discuss what Pippa means when she says, "Mrs. Lee had given me much more than her key" (p. 225). What is Jung-Hwa's role in the success of the party? How does the party help everyone, including Mina, have a merry Christmas?

11. Explain the symbolism of the golden scrunchie that Helen and Bianca give Pippa the day after the party. What causes Bianca to change? Compare Pippa and Bianca's relationship in *Pippa Park Crush at First Sight* to their relationship in *Pippa Park Raises Her Game*.

12. If you were to pick one character from *Pippa Park Crush at First Sight* who is most like you, who would it be and why? Who is most unlike you and why? Which character from the book would you want as your friend and why?

Q&A with Author Erin Yun

Did you draw from your own experiences when you wrote *Pippa Park Crush at First Sight*?

My mom is Korean, and my dad is a mix of Polish and Germanic. In the book, the protagonist is a Korean American girl, and a lot of her favorite things—from her love of walnut cakes filled with red bean to the Korean drama *Boys Over Flowers*—were my favorite things growing up, as well. In *Pippa Park Crush at First Sight*, Pippa worries that her best friends will grow apart from her now that they are in a relationship with each other. As someone who didn't date until college, I could relate to Pippa's insecurities that her friends might care more about their romantic relationships than their platonic ones, as well as the internal pressure she feels to "keep up" with her friend group.

How did you come up with the characters?

One of the most fun things about drafting the book was deciding which characters from *Great Expectations* would become which characters in *Pippa Park Raises Her Game*, and how the updated characters would diverge from the originals. Some of the first characters that made it into the book (besides Pip/Pippa, of course!) were Biddy (now Buddy), Joe (now Jung-Hwa), and Estella (now Eliot).

Who is your favorite character in the book?

I guess this question depends on the definition of *favorite*. Since the book is written in first person, I spent so much time in Pippa's mind that I can't help but be a little partial toward her even if I'm also the most critical of her at times. On the other hand, I had so much fun writing Mrs. Lee's character (and her cat, Boz) that she has to be a top choice. Mrs. Lee made her first appearance in *Pippa Park Raises Her Game*, and while I didn't intend for her to be a central character in the sequel, her enthusiastic, fun-loving personality captured my heart. Even though it takes some time for Pippa to warm up to her older neighbor, I was a fan of Mrs. Lee from page one.

Tell us more about the process of creating Pippa Park's character.
Even before I started writing the book, I was already brainstorming Pippa's character. I would draw sketches of her, make playlists of songs I thought she would listen to, and take personality quizzes for her. (She's an ESFP in case anyone was wondering.) I would also just daydream random conversations where she was talking to her friends or her teachers—anything that could let me get a feel for her voice.

Does she remind you of yourself at all?
Hmm, in some ways, yes. We both burst into tears during arguments, are terrible at math, and adore walnut cakes, for example. But I think we're quite different, as well. Pippa is more exuberant and bolder than I am, while I'm a little more introverted and more of a dreamer than she is. And while we both had a lot of crushes in middle school, when Pippa gets a crush, she crushes *hard*.

What inspired the key family relationship and dynamic between Jung-Hwa, Mina, and Pippa?

Jung-Hwa's relationship with Mina is based on many different inspirations: the relationship between Joe Gargery and Mrs. Gargery in *Great Expectations*, of course, but also the relationship between Jan-di's parents from one of my favorite Korean dramas growing up—*Boys Over Flowers*—with a touch of the dynamic between my own parents. As a kid, I always knew that the general rule was that if I wanted something big, like a new phone, my mom would be the most likely to say yes, but if I wanted something small, like a magazine or an ice cream, my dad was the person to go to.

Why did you become a writer?

There wasn't a particular reason; it's just something I've always done and always loved. I've been writing for longer than I can remember—first, in old notebooks with such terrible handwriting that no one, not even myself, would ever be able to decipher it, and then later, on the family computer whenever I could fight off my siblings for computer time.

When you're having trouble writing, what do you usually do?

I like to listen to music and kind of just zone out. Once my mind relaxes, I can start to hear the conversations of the various characters hanging around my mind. It's often not the scene I'm working on. Sometimes, it's not even the characters I'm writing. But it helps to give me a creativity boost and a fresh perspective, and it lets me go back to the text feeling reenergized.

What do you like to do when you aren't writing?
I like debating, traveling (favorite places include Seoul, South Korea, and London, England), and playing games—I'm terrible at *Mario Kart* but unwisely competitive about it.

Korean Language Glossary and Pronunciation Guide

Seollal 설날 (sol-lahl) *noun*: Lunar New Year; a very important holiday in Korea when families pay tribute to ancestors and enjoy a feast with relatives; occurs in either late January or early February

aiegoo 아이고 (ah-ee-goo) *phrase*: Oh no! Oh dear! Oh my!

arasseo 알았어? (ah-rah-sso) *phrase*: as a tag question: Okay? Got it? All right?

bibimbap 비빔밥 (bee-bim-bahp) *noun*: a dish served in a large bowl with various vegetables *(namul)* mixed with rice and spicy pepper paste *(gochujang)* along with an egg and seasoned meat

dongtaejeon 동태전 (dohng-tay-juhn) *noun*: pollack fish cakes fried in egg batter, often served for special occasions along with other fried foods and side dishes

gangaji 강아지 (gahng-ah-jee) *noun*: a puppy or dog; in this case, it's used as a term of affection for a child

gwenchana 괜찮아 (gwen-chahn-nah) *phrase*: I'm fine; It's nothing; I'm all right; Okay.

Keuriseumaseu 크리스마스 (kuh-ree-suh-muh-suh) *noun:* Christmas

jal bonaeseyo 잘 보내세요 (jahl-bo-nay say-oh) *phrase:* Have a Merry Christmas!

kimbap 김밥 (ghim-bahp) *noun:* Korean-style sushi rolls filled with various items, such as crab, spinach, or tuna

kimchi 김치 (ghim-chee) *noun:* spicy fermented vegetables (often Napa cabbage) served with all Korean meals; the national dish of South Korea

kimchi-jjigae 김치찌개 (ghim-chee-jee-gae) *noun:* a spicy kimchi-based stew made with a variety of ingredients such as scallions, tofu, pork, or seafood

kkori gomtang 꼬리 곰탕 (ggo-ree gohm-tahng) *noun:* a Korean-style, slow-simmered oxtail soup. Ingredients include *gochugaru*, daikon radish, scallions, soy sauce, and more.

Omma (Eomma) 엄마 (uhm-ma) *noun:* Mom or Mommy

yeobo 여보 (yuh-bo) *noun:* a term of endearment for one's spouse

---

Romanization source:
http://roman.cs.pusan.ac.kr/input_eng.aspx

Acknowledgments

Wow. Here we are again! When I wrote the acknowledgments for *Pippa Park Raises Her Game*, I was undeniably excited but also worried that I wouldn't have room to give a personal thank you to each and every person who helped mold the book into its final shape. So please know that, like its predecessor, *Pippa Park Crush at First Sight* would not exist without the immense support system that helped bring it to life. From editing to marketing to emotional support, there are dozens of people who made this book possible, and I am so grateful to each one of you.

Tracey, Eloise, and Susan: Thank you, thank you, and one more thank you for the tremendous amount of work you devoted to this book! I value all your suggestions, edits, and advice immensely, and was often humbled by your insights. Thank you for pushing me to be a better writer. On the flip side—an equally big shout-out to Stacey, Nicole, Sam, and Dienesa for all the support and enthusiasm you have given to Pippa Park. Thank you for going above and beyond in your efforts to connect Pippa Park with readers. I am also grateful to Jaime, Ellen, Bev, Debra, and everyone else who helped transform *Crush at First Sight* from a draft into a real-life novel! You are all magical.

To my family: I love you infinitely. Thank you for your endless encouragement and for always supporting my writing. Mom, you inspire me with your strength and your work ethic. Dad, you inspire me with your compassion and warmth. Thank you both for not only buying dozens of copies of my book but also convincing random strangers to take a chance on it as well. Natalie, Daniel: Thank you for being the best siblings ever. These past few years have been hard for everyone, and I'm so grateful to have a solid support system backing me up. Speaking of which: a giant shout-out to my friends. Thank you for being patient when I would text the group chat with random writing questions at weird hours of the night, and for cheering me up and giving me momentum when I felt uninspired. And Alex, I can't emphasize enough how important you are to both me and my writing. I'm so lucky to have a partner who is endlessly supportive, kind, and encouraging, and who keeps three different copies of my debut novel on his desk. I love you.

And finally—heaps of gratitude to my readers. Thank you for taking a chance on this book, a chance on Pippa Park, and a chance on me. Truly, it means the world to me.

About the Author:
Erin Yun grew up in Frisco, Texas, and used to play basketball as a middle grader. She received her BA in English from New York University and is currently pursuing her Masters in Creative Writing at Cambridge. She developed the Pippa Park Author Program, an interactive writing workshop, which she has conducted in person and virtually at schools, libraries, and bookstores.

About Fabled Films & Fabled Films Press
Fabled Films is a publishing and entertainment company creating original content for young readers and middle-grade audiences. Fabled Films Press combines strong literary properties with high quality production values to connect books with generations of parents and their children. Each property is supported by websites, educator guides and activities for bookstores, educators, and librarians, as well as videos, social media content and supplemental entertainment for additional platforms.

FABLED FILMS PRESS
NEW YORK CITY

fabledfilms.com

Connect with Fabled Films and the *Pippa Park Book Series*:
www.PippaPark.com
www.fabledfilms.com
Facebook: @Fabled.Films.Press | Instagram: @fabled.films
Twitter: @fabled_films